The
PROJECT

The
PROJECT

Gail Vinall

Scripture Union
130 City Road, London EC1V 2NJ

By the same author for older readers:
Stand Out in a Crowd
Mirror Image

First published 1989

ISBN 0 86201 561 8

Phototypeset by Input Typesetting Ltd, London
Printed and bound in Great Britain by Cox and Wyman Ltd, Reading

Chapter One

The removal van arrived at ten o'clock. John was
sure of that because his new digital watch played
the James Bond theme tune on the hour and it had
just finished when the huge lorry pulled up on next
door's drive. Two men in overalls jumped down
from the cab and opened the huge doors at the
back by sliding three massive bolts. The tailboard
was mechanically operated and for the next hour it
whirred up and down with bits of furniture on it.

John watched most of the operation over the
garden fence, his toes in two knot-holes in the
wood. He hooked his elbows over the top and
practised body lifts by sometimes releasing his toes
and dangling on his skinny arms until they hurt.
Meanwhile, beds, chairs, cases, a fridge and several
boxes marked 'FRAGILE' came out of the lorry and
disappeared round the back of the house.

Mrs Sampson had moved out ages ago. John

had liked her. She used to give him and his sister, Sarah, handfuls of ripe cherries from her tree, and she had been a favourite babysitter. Mind you, that had been a long time ago. Last Christmas Mum had told John that Mrs Sampson was too old to babysit any more and ever since then Angela, who was sixteen and lived across the road, had stayed with them instead, when Mum and Dad went out. Then Mrs Sampson fell ill and Mum had kept popping round to do shopping or take some soup for the old lady. Finally, Mrs Sampson had to go and live in an old people's home in Brighton. That was a long way away but Mum and Dad said it was the best plan because Mrs Sampson would have company and be looked after. So she had gone, only there hadn't been a great big removal van because she only needed to take clothes and books to the home in Brighton. The house had stayed empty for months. Dad said it wouldn't sell because it needed so much work done on it. The garden certainly did. It was a jungle now – much nicer than theirs. If only John and Sarah had been allowed to go round there, they could have had fantastic games of hide and seek or pirates in the undergrowth. Now of course, whoever was moving in would cut everything down again. Just who *was* moving in? John could only see the two men in overalls with the name of the removal company printed across their backs. It was probably someone old, John decided, because there hadn't been any cots or toys or racing bikes in the big van – just boring settees, gardening equipment and potted plants. John was pleased that he had remembered these items and made such a brilliant logical conclusion. It was his well-tuned detective mind, of course. He and his sister were both going to be policemen when they grew up. Well, Sarah would be a WPC and John would be a famous detective. All the serious crimes in the country would be solved by Chief Inspector John Ward, and there was no harm in starting some detecting right now. John liked inventing games and planning adventures. The case would be to solve the mystery of the missing next door neighbours. . . .

John was disturbed from his detection by the arrival of his twin sister, Sarah. Unlike John she could be very noisy and always wanted to rush at things, but together they were excellent friends and could spend hours without falling out. They still sat next to each other at school, just as they had in infant class.

Sarah had been to have her hair cut with Mum in town and, after sitting still for so long, she burst into the garden like a human rocket, shouting John's name.

'I'm here!' he called, sliding down from his perch.

'Your jeans are all green,' Sarah remarked.

John looked down at the mossy streaks from the fence which started at his stomach and reached to his knees. They both wore jeans and red checked shirts but, as usual, John couldn't keep tidy for long.

'Mum'll go mad when she sees them,' his sister added with relish.

'You've had your hair cut, basin head,' John teased, just to annoy her a bit.

Sarah shook her brown hair crossly. 'Well, it's

better than your spikes. Anyway, what have you been doing?'

'Observing,' John replied, mysteriously.

'What?'

'Next door. The furniture is all in now but the neighbours are missing. I'm working out what sort of people they are.'

'It's not they, it's him,' Sarah corrected. 'We saw him get out of his car as we arrived and Dad introduced himself. They're still talking, I think. His name's Mr Linden.'

John frowned. It was always the same. As soon as a real mystery happened, Sarah had to ruin things by finding out a perfectly sensible solution to the problem.

'He's got a limp, though,' Sarah added, 'so that's a sort of mystery, I suppose.'

'Yeah!' John agreed, his blue eyes sparkling as he imagined a dozen daring situations Mr Linden must have been in to come by the injury.

'Right then!' he announced. 'We're going to stalk Mr Linden for the rest of the morning. Go and get your notebook so we can take down any evidence.'

Sarah trotted indoors to find paper and a pen. It didn't matter that John was always pretending to be a detective and making everybody seem like criminals, when they never were, just so long as they had fun crawling round the garden spying. Mr Linden came down his drive, next to John's lookout on the fence ten minutes later, so the twins lay on their stomachs wriggling along the ground keeping him in sight through the gaps in the fence.

'He mustn't see us yet!' John hissed when Sarah

tried to stretch her legs by standing up.

'Why not?' Sarah whispered back.

'He'll know he's being watched and stop what he's doing.'

'But he isn't *doing* anything out of the ordinary yet!'

'He might, if he thinks he's safe,' John explained. 'Right, over to the tree house. . . . Go!'

They ran full pelt across the lawn and climbed the rope ladder before Mr Linden who had disappeared inside, came out again. The tree house, built by Dad, was a perfect lookout over next door's garden. It had plastic windows and was built on a platform jutting out from the main trunk so even in summer the leaves and branches didn't get in the way. Inside, the twins could just stand up, but it was a bit cramped since John had moved in all his old comics and Sarah her sketchboard. They took it in turns to keep lookout but there wasn't very much to report. Mr Linden just did all the usual things a man moving into a new house might do. He carried empty packing crates out to the garage, opened windows upstairs, wandered around the garden a bit and kept popping in and out of the back door.

After a while, Sarah got bored of watching and picked up her sketch board. She was good at drawing and soon produced a head and shoulders sketch of Mr Linden. It showed his eyes with bushy eyebrows, his beard with grey streaks, and the brown sweater he had on. Sarah's tongue stuck out a little as she concentrated on the picture. All the way round, she drew a line in thick black felt tip pen, then she carefully printed the man's name underneath and at the top, in block capitals, WANTED!

'There, that's our identikit photo,' Sarah announced, peeling off the sheet and handing it to John.

He squinted at the drawing and then nodded, pleased. 'We'll stick it up on the wall so we can refer to it when we bring him in for questioning.'

'What about?'

'His limp, of course.'

'I don't know,' Sarah said thoughtfully. 'He might not want to remember about it if it was painful or something. It might be rude – you know, like Mum says, about not staring at people if there's something wrong with them.'

Sarah was sensitive about people's feelings. After being a policewoman, Sarah thought she might like to be a nurse so she could make people feel better when they were ill.

There wasn't a chance to discuss this any more however, because something had suddenly caught John's eye and he was squeaking excitedly.

'What's up! Let me see,' Sarah said, pushing him away from the window.

'Shh!!' John whispered, rather loudly.

Below them, Mr Linden was standing with a pair of binoculars held to his eyes. He was fiddling with the focus and turning very slowly, as if to get a good look at the entire garden. The twins stared, wondering what he could see through the lenses or what he might be looking for. Then quite deliberately, they saw Mr Linden turn towards *their* garden and the next moment they were looking straight into the two glass eyes of his binoculars.

12

'Duck!' John hissed, throwing himself onto the comics. After the long morning of spying they really were quite shocked at the thought that Mr Linden had been watching them too. They lay on the dark floor of the tree house, their hearts pounding.

'Did he see us?' Sarah asked.

'Not sure.'

'Let's look again.'

'No, wait!' John commanded.

They held their breath for what seemed like hours but was probably less than a minute, then slowly crawled back up to the window. Mr Linden was gone.

'Oh, we've missed him,' Sarah sighed.

'Never mind – at least we know we're really on to something now.'

'What do you mean?' Sarah asked.

'Well, he *must* be suspicious, mustn't he, if he spends his time spying on all the neighbours with binoculars? He could be a thief, waiting to burgle us all, or a member of a desperate gang.'

'He might just like looking at things, like Grandad when we go out for walks.'

'Grandad looks at the view and there isn't a view from next door. It's just gardens and houses. No, he's definitely up to something strange.'

'John and Sarah, it's dinner-time. Come in and get washed!' Their dad's voice floated up to them.

Mr Linden had obviously gone inside and in any case, the twins were starving.

'Dad, how far can you see with binoculars?' John asked, as he ate a second helping of beefburgers.

'It all depends on how strong the lenses are –

but several hundred metres usually.'

'And can you see things really clearly?'

'Oh yes, as if they were a hand's reach in front of you.'

Mr Ward smiled at the twins. He wondered why that question had suddenly popped up and knew that, if he asked, John would probably come up with another of his fantastic stories.

'Are we going out this afternoon, Dad?' Sarah asked, between mouthfuls.

'I must finish painting the front window, love, so I'm afraid you'll have to amuse yourselves.'

'That's all right,' John replied at once, which surprised Mr Ward. Usually John was anxious to go out at the weekend.

'Mr Linden seems very nice,' Mum said and at once the twins stopped chewing, expecting some extra information.

'Yes, he comes from somewhere up north, near Derby I think he said,' Dad added.

'Is he married?' Sarah asked.

'It doesn't look like it. He didn't mention a wife when I was talking to him earlier.'

'Well, I think I'll invite him round for coffee later this evening,' Mum decided as she started to stack the dishes. 'It's never much fun spending your first night in a new house surrounded by cases. I'm glad we've got a neighbour at last.'

John was amazed. How could his mum invite the stranger to their house without knowing a thing about him? He might stake out their whole house and have leaked the information to a gang of thieves by tomorrow morning.

'Are you going to finish the custard or not?' Mum asked, her hand hovering above the bowl.

'What? Oh yes!' John said, coming back to reality. He spooned out the rest of the custard eagerly but his mind was still working on plans to catch Mr Linden, just as soon as they found out what he was up to.

Once they had helped to dry the plates, John and Sarah were free to do what they wanted. They made for the tree house first of all but there was no sign of Mr Linden.

'He must be having lunch too,' Sarah decided.

John took the sketch down and added a pair of binoculars, slung around the neck of their suspect. Then he made a list of the things they had found out about Mr Linden.

'How do you spell "distinguishing"?' John said, his pencil poised over the paper.

Sarah thought a minute and then said, 'Just write "dist." for short. They always do that on forms.'

'Right, dist. features − a limp.' John wrote this carefully and then stuck the sheet back up on the wall with a drawing pin.

'What now?' Sarah said, rolling onto her stomach and flicking through a comic idly. 'I want to do something exciting.'

'We've got to keep him under observation,' John said.

'But we *have* and he isn't going to do anything to-day. He's probably unpacking. Why don't we . . .'

'Shh!' John interrupted suddenly and grabbed Sarah's arm. 'Look! It's him!'

Mr Linden was carefully locking the back door.

He had a raincoat over one arm and a brown wallet sticking out of his back trouser pocket.

'He's going to have a rendezvous!' John exclaimed.

'What's that?'

'A meeting with his gang – to plan their next crime.'

'Oh, he's going out!' Sarah moaned. 'And now we'll never know where to.'

'It's all right, he's not taking the car! Come on – we'll follow him.'

'We can't just go out, John.'

'We'll ask Mum if we can go to the shops for her, come on.'

They scuttled down the ladder and across the lawn, almost tripping each other up in the race to be first.

'Mum!' they both shouted. 'Can we go to the shops for you?'

'What? Now? Oh, do wipe your feet, both of you, before you stomp grass all over my clean floor.'

The twins retreated to the back door mat, hopping up and down impatiently.

'Please Mum, we want to go to the shops.'

'Why now, all of a sudden?'

John could have exploded. Why did his mum have to ask silly questions when they were in such a hurry?

'It's part of our game, Mum,' Sarah explained patiently. 'We're detecting this criminal and . . .'

'Oh no, not more police work!' Mum groaned.

'Can we go, just down to the shops please?' John pleaded.

Mum reached for her purse and took out a pound coin. 'You can fetch me six apples and a nice packet of biscuits for coffee tonight. If there's any change you can divide it between you for sweets.'

'Oh great, Mum!' Sarah said, holding out her hand, but John was already half-way down the drive.

'Come straight back!' Mum called after them.

'OK,' Sarah replied for them both. She ran down the drive and out onto the pavement just in time to see John's fair head disappear around the corner. Putting on an extra spurt Sarah pounded down their road and then turned left into Pear Tree Drive. This was a slightly wider road and at the bottom was a row of shops. They were allowed to walk there on their own because they didn't have to cross any roads. It took only ten minutes to walk and the twins could run it in far less time. At intervals along the road were huge chestnut trees. These produced bags of conkers in autumn; last year the twins had collected over a hundred to take to school for their friends to share.

Suddenly Sarah spotted John, crouched behind one of the massive tree-trunks. He saw her coming and beckoned to her to slow down. She tiptoed over and crouched beside him. John pointed around the trunk and Sarah saw that Mr Linden had stopped about twenty-five yards further up the road. He was studying an envelope but in a while he put the paper back in his pocket, slung the raincoat over his shoulder and strolled on.

The twins waited for him to get a little way ahead, then rushed to the next tree. It would have been less conspicuous to walk calmly behind him, but John liked to be dramatic.

At last they reached the shops. Mr Linden went into the chemist so John ran off to get the apples and biscuits from the Spar shop while Sarah wandered up and down keeping watch. She saw their neighbour come out of the chemist and then head for the post office. He was only just in time because Mrs Priddle, the postmistress, was closing the awning over the shop window with a long metal pole.

John came out of the Spar shop, the apples bashing against his legs as he hurried back to Sarah.

'He's in there,' Sarah pointed and then pretended to be tying her shoe. These were tricks she and John had practised for not attracting attention when they were waiting for a suspect.

'What's he doing?' John said, when Mr Linden hadn't reappeared ten minutes later. Sarah shrugged her shoulders.

'We could choose our sweets while we're waiting,' she suggested.

John had almost forgotten about the change in his pocket, but despite the temptation he wasn't going to be put off the case. Just then, the Post Office door swung open and Mr Linden came out carrying a large oblong parcel, wrapped in brown paper. He tucked it under his arm, looked up and down the road and moved off.

Sarah and John had turned their backs while he went past but they had both seen the parcel and both had their ideas about what it contained.

'Looked like a book,' Sarah declared.

'No way, too big,' John said.

'Well, what then?' Sarah asked.

'A walkie talkie maybe. That would fit into a box that size.'

'So would lots of things. Let's choose some sweets.' Sarah had already lost interest. John thought about following Mr Linden back but he was obviously going home so there wasn't much point. Anyway, they had twenty-nine pence to divide equally so it was going to take a bit of thinking about. The chews at two for a penny usually sorted those problems out though. They went into the newsagent's, mouths watering.

A little later, they wandered slowly back home, chewing seriously. On the way, they chatted about the pictures they had to finish to go up on the church notice board the next day, and Mr Linden was forgotten.

'I'm going to colour mine,' Sarah decided.

'I'm not, it spoils it, I think,' John replied.

'I hope Mrs Williams lets me do the title with her stencil,' Sarah said.

'You did it last time.'

'I know but she said I did it really neatly.'

'Yes, but someone else might want to have a go this time.'

'Do you, then?'

'No, but someone else in the class might.'

Sarah sighed. John was right of course, but it was really hard to share sometimes when you wanted to do something very badly. Mrs Williams had talked about sharing last week in Sunday School. They had played a game where you had to give away counters if you landed on a certain square. In the end everyone had the same number, even though they'd all started off with different numbers. That had been fun. Some things were more difficult though.

John finished his chew and stuffed the wrapper into his jeans pocket. They could see Dad on the ladder just finishing the painting.

'Hey, Dad, can you play football with us now?' John called.

'All right, just give me a minute to wash these brushes.'

The afternoon raced by with games, tea and then, for a treat, a Walt Disney video before they had their baths.

Mum came up to say goodnight. John sat on Sarah's bed while they prayed together then went into his own room to read for a while.

'Don't be long before you put off the light, you two,' Mum called from the landing.

'OK.'

'Hey, Mum!'

'What now?'

'When is Mr Linden coming?' Sarah asked, suddenly remembering.

'About nine o'clock. You'll be asleep by then.'

No, I won't, John thought as he snuggled down under the duvet.

As soon as it was quiet downstairs John tiptoed into Sarah's room and shook her.

'Uh, what?' she mumbled.

'Come on! We're going to spy!'

They settled themselves on the landing and

waited. After a while the front door bell chimed. A ray of light shot across the downstairs hall as Dad came out of the lounge. Coffee smells wafted up to the twins as they leant against the bannisters trying to get a peep at the visitor. Mr Linden said, 'Good evening' in a deep growly sort of voice and shook hands with their dad, but before they could get a proper look the adults had gone back into the lounge and closed the door.

'I'm cold,' Sarah grumbled and slid back into bed.

John was going to stay awake until Mr Linden left but a long time before that, sleep overtook him. The last thing he heard was his mum's laugh and their neighbour's deep voice.

Chapter Two

The first thing the twins did on a Sunday morning was to go downstairs and make their parents a cup of tea. It had become a custom now so Mr and Mrs Ward wouldn't get up until they'd had their morning cuppa.

Sarah was putting milk in the mugs when John wandered into the kitchen. Paddy, their cat, was sitting on the floor flicking her tail to and fro. John took out the box of cat biscuits and poured some into the red cat bowl. Paddy jumped up and rubbed herself against his pyjama legs at once.

'Mum says that's just cupboard love,' Sarah said.

'What's cupboard love?' John wondered.

'It's when you only like someone when they give you something nice.'

'Oh, you're not like that, are you, Paddy?' John said, tickling her ears. Paddy was crunching the hard biscuits and making crumbs all over the doormat.

Sarah balanced the mugs carefully on a tray and waited for John to go ahead and open the doors. Their parents were awake, because the twins could hear them talking but they always pretended to be asleep when the twins reached their door.

John knocked softly. Mr Ward groaned and mumbled, 'Come in,' at which point John rushed into the room as if it was part of an SAS attack. It was the same every week but still good fun. Once the tea was drunk the twins used the bottom of the double bed like a trampoline until their parents had had enough and abandoned their ideas of a lie-in.

Church was at eleven o'clock and there were lots of jobs to be done before that. Mr Ward liked to disappear into his greenhouse. He said he had to spray the tomatoes and check the cuttings but John had seen him just sitting in the tatty old deckchair on lots of mornings. The twins couldn't understand why grown-ups liked to sit still and do nothing at all whenever they could.

This morning Sarah was helping to make an apple pie. Mrs Ward had chopped all the apples up and weighed the ingredients but Sarah had learned to mix pastry and roll it out, so she always did it if there was time. John didn't think Sarah was as good at it as their mum but he didn't say so.

John swiped a piece of apple from the dish as he went past the kitchen table. Sarah flicked his hand with a spoon but he was too quick and escaped before she could take aim. Then he teased Paddy in the garden for a while, until the poor cat jumped over the fence and ran off to find some peace. He wished he'd stayed awake long enough to see Mr Linden the night before. His mum and dad hadn't said anything about him that morning. John stared at the upstairs window thoughtfully. The blinds were still closed, so Mr Linden must still be in bed. 'He can't be coming to church then,' John thought. Mrs Sampson always had. In fact they used to give her a lift. John suddenly remembered his drawing for Miss Williams and went to find it. As he passed the greenhouse he saw the top of his dad's head in the deckchair.

'Busy, Dad?' he called out as he went by.

Mr Ward jumped slightly before sinking back down into his chair. John laughed.

It was always the same on Sundays. They started out really peacefully and then got into a panic just before church. Mr Ward came wandering into the kitchen still in his gardening shirt just as Mrs Ward set the timer on the oven for their lunch and dashed upstairs to do her hair. The twins would be quite all right, not bothering anyone and then both adults would pick on them.

'Sarah, have you combed your hair?'

'John, have you brushed your teeth?'

Then they would start at each other.

'Sheila, I can't find my blue tie.'

'It's where you left it.'

'No, it isn't!'

Then it was back to them.

'Sarah, have you cleaned your shoes?'

'No Mum!'

'Why not?'

'Because I'm wearing my trainers.'

John and Sarah sighed and looked at each other. It was awful to have such disorganised parents. They went out to the car and waited. Five minutes later their parents came rushing down the path, Mr Ward tugging at his tie irritably.

It was only a five-minute drive to church and Mrs Ward was always saying they ought to walk but they hardly ever did.

When they arrived, the twins collected hymn books while their parents talked to people at the door. Everyone said 'hello', and made the twins feel welcome. Soon, they caught sight of Katie and Paul, who were friends of theirs from school.

For the first ten minutes everyone stayed together in church. It was all right, because it didn't last long, but John wasn't too keen on singing hymns. It was more interesting when the vicar told them a story and asked for volunteers to come and hold things for him. Sarah was always volunteering to do things like that but John preferred to watch. This morning, the vicar was talking about losing valuable things, and finding them. He had an old gold watch on a chain, which he let Paul hold while he told the story. Perhaps he would be able to see it close up after the service, John thought.

After another hymn, all the children went out of a side door which led to the hall where they had their lessons. John and Sarah were in class two. Mrs Williams led them into their room where chairs and tables had been set out in a semi-circle.

'Oh good – we're potato printing!' Sarah said excitedly as they crowded into the room. It was only when they had sat down that the twins realised there was a new boy. He was quite tall, with red curly hair and lots of freckles all over his face. Sarah said 'Hello', but he didn't reply. Maybe he hadn't heard.

'Ah now, this is Jamie,' said Mrs Williams, putting her hand on his shoulder. 'Let's introduce ourselves, and make Jamie feel welcome.'

Jamie didn't look as if he wanted to be made very welcome. In fact, John reckoned he was really fed up about being here at all. The new boy had the same look on his face that John did when he was told tht he couldn't stay up to watch football because it was too late, a sort of mix between sad and angry.

'I don't like him,' Sarah murmured in John's ear when Mrs Williams was giving out the pots of paint a bit later.

John shrugged his shoulders. Sarah didn't always understand boys when they were in a mood. Jamie was definitely in a mood.

They said a prayer and then Mrs Williams collected the drawings they had started last week and complimented everyone on their colouring or neatness. A girl called Emma was picked to do the stencilling and Sarah hid her disappointment. They listened to a Bible story about a woman who swept out her house to find a coin she had dropped and was so pleased to find it that she gave all her friends a party to celebrate. Mrs Williams said that God felt just as happy when children or grown-ups said that they loved him, because it was as if he had found them. It was a good story and everyone was quiet, listening. Even Jamie stopped fidgetting but then, at the end, he suddenly said in a loud voice, 'I don't believe in God.'

For a moment no-one said a thing. Sarah thought Mrs Williams would be cross but the teacher just smiled and said, 'Well, perhaps you don't, Jamie, but I believe God is real and that he cares about all of us. That means you too, whether you believe in him or not.'

Sarah was confused. She had always imagined that everyone believed in God if they came to church.

From that point on, Jamie seemed determined to be awkward. He didn't want to do any printing and sat on his own, scowling. Sarah asked him if she could use his potato half and when he didn't reply she took it. Just as she had loaded it with a thick layer of orange paint, Jamie reached over and grabbed it back, flicking paint over the table.

'Give it back!' Sarah yelled.

'It's mine,' sneered Jamie.

'You weren't using it.'

'Well I am now.'

'You are not!' Sarah leaned across the table to snatch it back just as Mrs Williams turned round. The potato flew out of her hand, landing face down in the middle of her picture.

'Sarah, I'm surprised at you!' Mrs Williams said. 'Please ask each other if you want to borrow things – don't just snatch . . . and look at the mess you've made!'

'It wasn't me,' Sarah began but Jamie's smirking face stopped her. Hot tears came up and she had to swallow hard to keep them down. John helped her clear up the table with a paper towel but the picture was a soggy mess and ended up in the bin. The morning was ruined for Sarah and she couldn't wait for the lesson to end. As for the new boy, she *hated* him.

'Aren't you very hungry?' Mrs Ward said as they ate lunch that day. Sarah was pushing peas and mushrooms round her plate slowly.

'She's in a mood because Mrs Williams told her off,' John grinned.

Mr Ward gave him a warning look.

'Do you want to tell us about it, Sarah?' Mum asked.

'I hate him and it's all his fault my picture got spoiled,' Sarah burst out.

'Who are you talking about?'

'Jamie,' John said, because Sarah's face was looking all hot and puffy again.

After a bit of encouragement from Mum, Sarah managed to explain about the awful morning.

'I don't expect he meant to get you into trouble,' Mr Ward said, wiping his mouth with a napkin.

'Yes, he did!' Sarah flared back. 'He's horrible, and so is Mrs Williams!'

'I thought you liked Mrs Williams?'

'Well, she wasn't fair.'

'It sounds as if she didn't see what happened. But in any case, you did take Jamie's paint.'

'It wasn't his paint. . . .'

'All right, potato then,' Mr Ward agreed, 'and perhaps you shouldn't have done.'

Sarah pouted and put her elbows on the table.

'Did you apologise to Mrs Williams for making a mess?' Mum asked.

'No, why should I? It wasn't all my fault. Anyway Jamie didn't say sorry.'

'If Sarah doesn't want her apple pie, shall I eat it?' John offered.

'No,' Mrs Ward replied. 'Sarah may feel like it later.'

'I won't,' Sarah said, but her dad took the plate out of John's reach anyway.

Once lunch was over Sarah went up to her room and closed the door. John didn't bother her. Girls were a bit funny when they'd been told off. He wouldn't have cared about the stupid potato, or Jamie, come to that. He couldn't understand why Sarah was in such a mood over a little thing like that. Now if something really awful had happened, like breaking your penknife or the batteries on your Walkman running out, then it would be quite reasonable to go on hunger strike, but over this, it seemed daft.

He wished Sarah would get over it, because he wanted her to keep a lookout for Mr Linden again. There was movement next door in the garden. John made for the tree house.

Upstairs Sarah was fighting with herself. She would have liked to phone up Mrs Williams and say sorry, because she liked her really, but she also wanted Jamie to be made to say sorry as well. He hadn't been told off at all and that was unfair. Sarah liked things to be perfectly fair. She was also cross that John hadn't stood up for her. He had just thought it was funny.

Mum came into her room with some clean clothes which she started to put away in Sarah's wardrobe.

After a while she sat on the bed and put her arms round Sarah's shoulders.

'Come on, love, cheer up,' she smiled.

'I hate him,' Sarah said, frowning.

'That isn't very nice.'

'Nor is he!'

'I don't like to hear you saying that you hate people.'

'Why shouldn't I say it if it's true?'

'Hate is a very strong thing and we've just been to church to learn about Jesus and how much he loves us. He wouldn't be very happy to hear you saying that you hate Jamie, would he?'

'I don't hate Jesus, just Jamie.'

'Jesus said that if we love him then we must try to be friends with each other.'

'After what happened this morning?'

'I think that was a bit of a misunderstanding. Perhaps Jamie was feeling cross today, so he took it out on you. You and John do that sometimes.'

'He said he doesn't believe in God,' Sarah remembered.

'Then you can try to show him that God is real, by being the sort of person who lives like Jesus did. That means forgiving people, even if they have been mean to us.'

'Well, I can't forgive Jamie because I don't know where he lives.'

'You can still forgive him in there,' Mum smiled, tapping Sarah's head gently. 'And you can say sorry to Mrs Williams right away. I don't expect she's feeling very happy about this morning either.'

Sarah sighed and then nodded. They went down-

31

stairs to phone up Mrs Williams. It was very easy talking to her. She made Sarah feel very grown up and sensible. Funnily enough, almost the moment the call was over, Sarah felt hungry again.

Mum handed Sarah the plate with the apple pie on. It had an extra large dollop of double cream on it. With the last bit of crust in her hand, Sarah wandered out into the garden. She felt in a much better mood now and even thought she could forgive John for laughing at her.

He was waving excitedly at her from the tree house and pointing into next door's garden. Sarah clambered up the ladder to join him.

'What is it?'

'Look, it's him and he's crawling around in the bushes.'

'Where?' Sarah said, unbelieving.

'There!'

Sure enough Mr Linden was on his hands and knees under the bushes in the middle of his garden.

'What on earth is he playing at?' Sarah asked.

'He must be looking for something. I bet it's a clue or a secret message.'

'He could be looking for a place to bury his stolen goods,' Sarah suggested.

Mr Linden certainly was acting in a very peculiar way for a grown-up. He was getting filthy dirty but it didn't seem to worry him at all.

Suddenly he stopped crawling and started scraping in the grass. Whatever it was he had found, he seemed pretty excited about it. He took out a little plastic bag and put something inside it. Then he edged out of the undergrowth, backwards. His lame leg dragged a bit but he looked really pleased with his discovery.

'Do you think Mrs Sampson buried treasure in her back garden before she left?' Sarah asked.

'I don't see why. She must have known she wasn't coming back here, anyway she was too ill to go digging before she left.'

They didn't know what to add to the list of evidence they had made. John scribbled down the time and the place and just wrote 'DUG UP UNIDENTIFIED OBJECT', thinking that it sounded very police-like.

Later Dad suggested a drive out to the coast. It was a favourite trip, and Mum packed up a picnic tea to eat when they got there. Berryman Head was a well-known local spot. A winding lane led almost as far as the coastguards' station. There was a rough gravel parking area and from there it was possible to walk miles in either direction along the coast path or straight out to the head. A tiny chapel stood on the headland. St Michael's was a tiny rough stone building, with a grassy floor. Dad said they still had services in the summer months and people could even get married there if they wanted.

Some sailors had built it, hundreds of years ago, as a thank-you to God for saving them from rough seas. Nowadays it was a prominent landmark and helped sailors to navigate their way around the rocky coastline.

It had been warm in their garden at home but out on the head there was a cool breeze. The twins had brought their frisbee with them and spent nearly an hour twirling it to each other, trying to make the spinning path more accurate.

The coastguard station was manned and Dad's FM radio was picking up a lot of the radio calls between the ships out at sea and the coastguards. On such a clear fine day, John and Sarah couldn't imagine how any ship could mistake the clear sweep of the bay or the jutting rocks below the headland. They knew it could be a dangerous place but today the waves just splashed gently against the cliffs.

'Can we go out to the chapel?' Sarah asked when they'd got fed up with throwing the frisbee.

'All right, we'll go down. I think your mum would like to stay here.'

Mrs Ward was sitting comfortably on the rug and showed no signs of wanting to move.

The twins ran ahead down to the chapel. It was a well-worn track and quite safe but off to the left and right rocks tumbled down to the cliff face which dropped sheer into the sea. Hundreds of feet below, waves sparkled blue and white against the rocks. It was terrifying and beautiful at the same time.

Sarah held back until she could see her dad's tall figure emerging from between the bushes which edged the path. When he had caught up, she slid her hand into his warm safe one. All around them, cows munched and wandered slowly over the grassy slopes.

'Don't they ever fall over the edge?' Sarah asked thoughtfully.

'No, they aren't stupid. They know how far to go before it isn't safe. They've got four legs as well, which helps.'

'It's a long way down, isn't it?' Sarah said

cautiously.

Dad squeezed her hand. 'So long as you stay on the path, it's quite safe. But you must never run off away from the track. The ground can be very slippery and once you fall over, nobody can see you.'

Sarah shuddered. John had reached the chapel and was leaning out of one of the windows on his stomach. Dad and Sarah ran to join him. Even though the chapel appeared to be right on the edge of the cliff, the land slipped away on the other side and it was possible to climb down for about a hundred feet before reaching the real edge. They decided to retrace their steps, though, because going down meant a hard climb up again.

As they walked back inland, the twins saw the coastguard station, standing weather-beaten but solid.

'What do the coastguards do?' John asked.

'They look out to sea, and listen to their radio, so if any sailor needs help, they can phone for the lifeboat crew at Halen to go out and rescue the people.'

'Are the coastguards always there?' John asked.

'Not all the time at this station.'

'I'd like to be a coastguard,' Sarah said.

'It's a very worthwhile job I should think,' Dad agreed.

'How does the equipment work?' John asked.

'Sailors know they're on course in fine weather from the landmarks, but in the fog or rain, the radar at the coastguard station picks them up on a special machine. Then the coastguards can radio to the ship and tell the captain how to steer. Or, if the worst comes to the worst and the ship is in difficulties, they can phone for the lifeboat.'

'I wish we could go inside.'

'They're very busy. I expect you need a special invitation to look round.'

'Couldn't we get one?'

'Well, maybe one day.'

John and Sarah gazed at the small white building curiously. It looked like a little cottage from the outside, except for the great aerials strapped to its walls. It was exciting to think of all the equipment inside and the men keeping lookout for ships in danger. John had already made up his mind that one day he'd find a way to visit and explore the place properly.

Chapter Three

Although at the weekend John and Sarah were always the first awake and up, weekdays were quite different. On Monday mornings in particular they were still snuggling under their duvets long after Mum had called them down to breakfast. They both enjoyed school once they were there, but the prospect of it at the start of a new week was a bit daunting.

This morning John spent ages in front of the bathroom mirror wetting his hair down and then spiking it up with a brush, keeping his sister hopping around outside on the landing waiting to brush her teeth.

'John, hurry up!' she called impatiently.

'Coming,' he replied, without making any effort to hurry.

'Have we got swimming this afternoon?' Sarah shouted.

John frowned, trying to remember what their teacher had said on Friday afternoon. Yes, she had reminded them to bring their costumes and towels. Brightening at the thought, John dashed out of the bathroom, almost knocking Sarah over, and made for the airing cupboard.

'Hey! Don't take the red towel, that's mine,' Sarah protested.

'Tis not! Anyway I got it first.'

'Don't you two start squabbling,' Mum warned, coming up the stairs.

Sarah, who still wasn't dressed, decided she'd better get a move on, so John, grinning, tucked the red towel, which was the biggest, into his school bag.

Since she was the last ready, Sarah ended up sitting in the back of Mum's battered Escort while John belted himself into the front seat. Sarah tried to look forward to the day ahead. It hadn't gone very well so far. She had no way of knowing that worse was to follow.

On the way to school Mum decided to stop for petrol, because she was going straight on into town to do some shopping. Dulo Primary School was about three miles from home, too far to walk comfortably but no time at all in the car. This particular morning though, the traffic was rather heavy and Mum got stuck behind a minibus which stopped at least four times before it turned off.

'We're going to be late!' Sarah said.

'Oh dear,' Mum muttered, biting her lip.

'It's all right,' John said, quite happy at the thought of being late for school.

'It is not!' Mum insisted. 'Tomorrow you must get up on time, Sarah.'

Sarah was indignant at getting the blame but before there was a chance to protest, the old red Escort turned into Milburn Avenue and it was time to get out. John and Sarah dragged their swimming gear, bags and anoraks out of the car, said goodbye to their mum and slammed the car door shut.

'Have a good day!' Mum shouted. They waved and then made a dash for the school gates. One or two children were still arriving but most were already lined up in the playground ready to go inside. The morning bell must have already rung.

John and Sarah had to dodge in and out of mums pushing prams or buggies away from the school. John looked at the babies and toddlers enviously. They weren't old enough to be at school yet and had only come with a parent to deliver older brothers and sisters.

The twins joined the end of Class 3 line, red in the face and panting. Mrs Lucas quietened them down by raising a hand to her mouth. The chattering died away like a ripple and then they trooped into the cloakrooms. The twins' pegs were next to each other. They hung up their coats, pushed their swimming gear into the lockers underneath and then joined the knot of children hustling into the classroom.

It was a large airy room, with lots of metal-framed windows looking out over the playing fields, and radiators painted blue around the other three walls. The blackboard was always washed at the weekend so on Mondays it was a deep black colour. Sarah loved to see it like that before Mrs Lucas used the board rubber for the first time and smeared dusty chalk all over it. By Friday it would be dirty grey again.

Several children crowded round the tank to look at the tadpoles but John knew they wouldn't have grown legs yet, so he didn't bother. He was more interested in the stick insects on the other bench. He was hoping Sarah and he could get to take them home at half term to look after.

'Seats everyone!' Mrs Lucas called and gradually chairs were scraped back as people found their places.

John and Sarah were on yellow table, which was near the stick insects at the back of the room. It wasn't until the class had sat down that the twins realised why everyone was noisier and more restless than usual. Standing next to Mrs Lucas at the front of the room was a new boy.

'Oh no, not *him* again!' Sarah said, but it was.

Jamie stood, head down, with a glowering expression on his face, next to the teacher's desk.

Sarah felt a rush of anger inside her but when she caught John's eye and he grinned she calmed down again. John was amused because the only empty chair in the room was at yellow table. Mrs Lucas was already leading Jamie towards it. He slumped into the seat rather sulkily. At first he kept his head down and picked at the corner of his new exercise book but Sarah couldn't drag her eyes away from him and when he finally glanced up he recognised the twins at once.

'This is John and Sarah,' Mrs Lucas was saying.

'We've met,' Sarah announced, not very enthusiastically.

'Oh, I see. Well then, I had better make Jamie your responsibility for today. You can see that he finds the dinner hall, and the playground at breaktime.'

'Yes, miss,' John mumbled. Normally it would have been a great privilege – it was interesting meeting new people and showing them around – but Jamie was different. He looked so miserable that it seemed that school did not appeal to him any more than Sunday School had done.

The first lesson was Maths. Everyone had different coloured books to work from. Jamie was given a green book, which John and Sarah had finished last term. For a while he just stared at the pages and then he said, 'I haven't got a pencil.' John fetched him a sharp pencil from the beaker on the bench. He didn't say thank-you for anything, just took it without a word. John didn't mind. He supposed it was a bit tough starting a new school.

They worked away busily for several minutes before Jamie's pencil point snapped. It wasn't surprising, Sarah thought, from the way he'd been stabbing away with it. Thick black figures marched unevenly down two pages. He threw the pencil down in disgust and made a lot of noise getting up to fetch another one. Unfortunately the remaining pencils were blunt. He sat down.

'Got a sharpener?' he grunted.

John shook his head and returned to a tricky sum he was doing.

Sarah felt torn. She had a sharpener in her pencil

case but why should she offer it to this boy who didn't even try to be friendly, and especially after Sunday? She returned to her own work but the sight of Jamie just sitting there, his mouth all droopy, finally won.

'Here!' she said, tossing the sharpener under his nose. It bounced twice before Jamie caught it. The boy held the sharpener without moving for a while, then he carefully sharpened his pencil before sliding it back to her, without a word.

After that, he seemed to cheer up slightly. Mrs Lucas came over to check his work and said that he could go on to the next book within a fortnight at the rate he was going. Sarah saw Jamie looking at her Maths book and knew he was trying to work out how fast he'd need to go to overtake her. Well, he'd have to think again about that! Maths was Sarah's favourite subject and she was one of the quickest in the class.

The bell rang at last and Mrs Lucas let them go. It was breezy but warm in the playground. Sarah found Katie and joined her in a game of hopscotch. John could do the showing round. Hopefully Jamie would make friends with someone else and then they wouldn't have to bother about him any more. Sarah told Katie all about the weekend but she didn't mention their new neighbour. That was a secret between John and herself; it was detective work and that was quite separate from school games. Anyway, Katie would probably laugh and spoil it all.

Any hope of Jamie finding himself a friend seemed unlikely. Although John kept introducing him to his friends, all Jamie did was mooch around with his hands in his pockets. When he *did* speak, it wasn't the kind of comment to make him popular.

'That's a pathetic pass,' he said, when they were watching Steve and Kevin play football.

Later he grumbled about the state of the football nets. 'Rubbish – there's holes all over the place. It wasn't like this in my last school. . . 'My dad's a brilliant footballer,' Jamie announced as they moved away from the makeshift game.

'Oh really?' John replied.

'He could have been a professional.'

John tried to be interested, but whenever he mentioned *his* dad, Jamie either didn't listen or interrupted with 'Well, my dad says . . .'

It seemed to be the only subject he got enthusiastic about, and once he started there was no stopping him. John listened with as much patience as he could, to a list of all the things Jamie's dad could do; how fast his car was, how expensive his new compact disc player was, all the things he'd promised to buy Jamie for his birthday. . . .

John was glad when the bell for the next lesson rang.

'Come on – we'd better go in,' he said, hurrying back to the classroom.

Next lesson was English and Mrs Lucas told them all to listen very carefully because they would be starting a new project. Lots of hands went up, and several girls called out ideas but Mrs Lucas silenced them.

'You are to get into pairs and choose for your project a group of people who help us in some way in the community. Now, any ideas?'

'Nurses!' shouted Ruth Sands, who'd just been in hospital to have her tonsils out.

'Yes, any others?'

'Dustbin men!'

'Teachers!' There was a groan and Mrs Lucas smiled.

'Vets!' called out Katie.

'They don't help *people*,' argued Sam Potter.

'The vet helped our cat when she got sick and that's the same thing as helping us,' Katie replied.

'Yes, vets do an important job in the community,' Mrs Lucas agreed.

Soon, people were saying 'We'll do doctors' or 'I'm doing milkmen.'

Lots of pairs wanted to do the same thing but Mrs Lucas said there would be a prize, awarded at half term, for the most interesting and original project.

Sarah looked at John excitedly. 'What'll *we* do?' she said. It was taken for granted that they would work together. John had wanted to do Police but Kerry-Ann had already chosen that and her dad was a policeman, so she'd get loads of information for the project. No, it had to be something no-one else would think of.

'I've got it!' John hissed, nudging Sarah.

'What?'

'Coastguards!' John rubbed his hands together, delighted at his choice, and already brimming with plans for making theirs the best project in the class. There might even be a possibility of getting in to see the station at Berryman Head.

'Great!' Sarah said. She hadn't seen any books on coastguards in the school library, she wasn't even very sure what they did, apart from Dad's explanation yesterday, but it was definitely unusual. No-one else had mentioned it.

In their enthusiasm, the twins hadn't even noticed Jamie, his face all moody again, rocking backwards on his chair. There was an odd number on yellow table. The two other pairs had settled on an idea.

Mrs Lucas came over and crouched down beside Jamie. 'Well now, perhaps you can join up with a pair here,' she encouraged.

Sarah felt John tense beside her as he leant over the paper they'd been scribbling notes on. Rather ashamed, she crossed her fingers, hoping that Mrs Lucas wouldn't pick on them, but of course she did.

'John and Sarah, have you come up with an idea yet?'

'We want to do coastguards, Miss,' Sarah explained.

'Really! What a good idea. I hadn't thought of that.'

John blushed with pleasure, but the next moment came the dreaded request.

'Can Jamie join you, then? I think there'll be plenty of work to do researching for your project – enough for three.'

Sarah and John looked at each other. They understood each other perfectly without saying anything. Neither wanted to have Jamie in on the project but both knew it would be quite wrong and unkind to refuse. All the things Mum and Dad, plus

Mrs Williams, had ever said about sharing, offering friendship, treating people as you wanted to be treated, flashed through their minds. On the other hand they wanted to keep the idea to themselves.

'I don't care. I'll work on my own,' Jamie suddenly said.

Mrs Lucas hesitated, not quite sure what was going on between the three pupils. 'Well, if you're sure, Jamie. . . .'

'No, it's OK,' John interrupted. 'We'd like you to work with us – wouldn't we, Sarah?'

'What? Oh yes!' Sarah said. She understood why John had decided to include Jamie like that, and they generally backed each other up.

John knew that the other boy had sensed their rejection in the silence. It had happened only once to John, when he'd first started swimming and hadn't made very good progress. In Class 2 he'd been one of the last to swim. Sitting on the side waiting for his teacher, while his friends had been playing at the other end and laughing at him a bit, just in fun, had been an awful experience. He could still remember it. Pretending you didn't care, when it was obvious that you did, was very hard. Anyway, perhaps if Jamie thought that they wanted him to work with them, he'd be a bit grateful and a lot more friendly.

That was too much to ask, John discovered.

'Can you check the library for any books?' Sarah asked.

'I don't know where it is,' Jamie said, drawing squiggly lines around Sarah's notes.

She picked up the paper with a sniff and stamped

off to the library.

'Look, don't you like the idea?' John said when Sarah had gone.

Jamie shrugged his shoulders. ' 'S'all right. Don't know anything about it.'

'Well that's the point – we can find things.'

'Waste of time,' Jamie replied.

'Perhaps your dad'll know something about it,' John suggested. It wasn't meant to be sarcastic but it *did* sound like that when the words came out.

'Yeah, I expect he does!' Jamie said, as if daring John to contradict him.

'Well, ask him, then.'

'I will when I see him . . .' Jamie suddenly blushed, coughed and added 'I'll ask him tonight,' very fiercely.

John didn't understand the kid at all. What a funny thing to say, *when I see him*.

'My dad knows about practically everything, see!' Jamie added. with a scowl.

'All right. Keep your hair on.'

It was just as well that Sarah came back. 'Not much,' she sighed, flopping a couple of magazines which looked about fifty years old on the desk.

'If only we could get inside the station itself at Berryman Head,' John said, dreamily.

'Where's that?' Jamie asked.

'It's not far – Dad took us there on Sunday.'

'My dad . . .'

John covered his ears and pretended to be reading, elbows on the desk.

They didn't get much done that lesson but the twins were doubly determined to produce a fantas-

47

tic project. Mrs Lucas had suggested they write off for some up-to-date information and the school secretary would type their letter and post it. Meanwhile John was drawing a map from the tourist guide, to label the two coastguard centres in their area. It would make a good title page for their project. Sarah was designing an elaborate cover, with stencilled letters to make it look really professional. Jamie flicked through the magazines without much effect but, on the whole, he didn't annoy the twins too much. Somehow or other, it looked as if he'd decided to adopt them as his 'friends'.

After lunch, a battered old coach arrived outside the school gates to collect the children who were going swimming. Mrs Lucas had managed to find some swimming trunks and a spare towel for Jamie from the PE stores which he was told to wash and return to the school as soon as possible.

He sat next to another boy on the coach but they didn't seem to get on too well. After a whole day though, John and Sarah had had enough. It was a relief to end the afternoon with swimming at the town baths. Sarah was trying to earn her certificate for completing twenty-five metres in backstroke, together with Katie and Julie. They spent most of the hour racing each other, kicking up water furiously to gain an extra few seconds speed.

Jamie got into trouble for ducking the boy he'd been sitting next to on the coach. John heard Mr Graham, the PE teacher, shouting at him in the changing rooms afterwards. Jamie wasn't the least bit sorry, even though he had to apologise to the boy.

Afterwards, he stood alone, rubbing his ginger hair with the borrowed towel and muttering angry words under his breath, not quite loud enough for Mr Graham to hear. 'Load of cissies,' John heard him say.

On the way back to school, no one sat next to Jamie at all. Mrs Lucas, who looked as if she had a headache, didn't try to persuade anyone to swap places. John was behind the two teachers on the journey back and although he didn't mean to, he couldn't help overhearing some of the things they were saying.

'New boy settling?' Mr Graham asked.

'Hard to say. He's not a very likeable lad from what I can see,' Mrs Lucas said.

'Nasty temper.'

'Well perhaps it's understandable, with the problem at home.'

'Oh dear, like that, is it?' Then the teachers started talking about some meeting after school.

John didn't understand what he'd overheard and knew it hadn't been intended for his ears. He decided not to tell anyone, not even Sarah. In any case, there wasn't much to tell. It was perfectly true that Jamie wasn't a friendly sort of person. But what was the problem at home? Jamie hadn't given any clues about that.

John couldn't help himself – he was already imagining amazing things which Jamie might be keeping a dark secret. At this rate there would be two mysteries to clear up, and it was still only Monday. John hoped there would be a chance to do some more spying on Mr Linden before tea. If only his mum could be trusted to notice any strange comings and goings, but she never seemed to realise all the exciting things going on around her.

Minutes later, the coach groaned around the corner and stood shaking as if with the effort, while the children tumbled off. They were allowed to go straight home but those who were waiting to be collected had to go back inside the school gates.

John decided to chat to Jamie, who was standing alone, apparently looking for a car to appear.

'Is your mum coming?' he asked.

'Think so.'

'So is ours, only she's usually late.'

'Has she got a big car?'

John laughed. 'No, it's an old wreck.'

Jamie looked pleased. 'So is my mum's. But Dad's is fantastic,' he added quickly.

John grinned to himself – he'd been expecting that.

When a lady with short auburn hair and a brown jacket appeared at the gates John knew at once that it must be Jamie's mum. He nudged Jamie and pointed. Sarah came up to wait with John just then.

'Bye,' she called as Jamie headed off. He looked surprised that she'd bothered to say it.

Jamie ran off to the lady, who put her arm round his shoulders. Jamie pulled away, embarrassed, and then they seemed to have a quick conversation, during which Jamie pointed at the twins. Then he came running back to them.

'Mum says do you want to come to tea tomorrow? It's my birthday – only I'm not having a party 'cos I don't know anyone here yet. You don't have to,' he added quickly.

It was a funny sort of invitation, and the last thing they'd expected from Jamie.

'We'd have to ask Mum,' Sarah said.

'Yeah, I've got to take your phone number, Mum says, if you're coming. Well?'

The twins weren't sure what to say, but it seemed rude not to accept.

'Thanks,' they said, still a bit bewildered.

'What's your number?'

'41024.'

Jamie scribbled it down on the back of his hand.

'Right then, see you,' Jamie called, moving off. He hesitated then turned to look at them. The expression on his face was almost a smile.

Chapter Four

Mrs Ward was surprised to receive a phone call from Jamie's mum just after tea-time. The twins had mentioned the invitation but when they'd explained who Jamie was, Mrs Ward almost thought it was a joke. Still, the lady on the phone had sounded very keen that John and Sarah should come. It was agreed that the twins would be collected from school with Jamie, and Mr Ward could fetch them home later in the evening.

'Can't Jamie's dad bring us home?' John asked, thinking of the big fast car.

'Mrs Clark didn't mention her husband. Perhaps he works late.' She paused and then added, 'You do *want* to go, don't you?'

'Yes, course we do,' John replied, when his sister didn't say anything.

'Well, that's fine. I'm so glad you've sorted out your differences. We must invite Jamie back next week. . . .'

'Maybe,' John interrupted. They'd see how tomorrow went, he thought, before Jamie came back to their home.

Out in the tree house later on, Sarah couldn't help moaning a bit.

'It'll probably be awful. I wish we weren't going.'

'It's only for a couple of hours, and he can't be as bad at home as he is in school. Anyway I want to find out . . .' John stopped, a bit guilty.

'Find out what?' Sarah asked, not missing a thing.

'Nothing – just see where he lives, and if his dad really has got all the things Jamie's been going on about.'

'Who cares!' Sarah said. 'Do you think it's really his birthday?'

'If he said so . . .' The twins already knew that there was something about Jamie you couldn't quite trust. Not that he lied exactly, just sort of exaggerated.

'What'll we give him, then?' Sarah wanted to know. It was too late to go to the shops and anyway, they hardly knew him – so how could they tell what he liked?

'I know, we'll make something,' John decided, eyes sparkling. 'You can draw a card and I'll invent something fantastic.'

They rushed indoors to find cardboard and felt-tip pens. Sarah loved designing things and she drew a really nice picture of a dog on roller-skates, copied from a cartoon in the paper. Mum found an envelope which fitted and Sarah used huge elaborate letters to write inside the card. She felt very pleased with the result but couldn't help wishing it was for a real friend who would appreciate it. The way Jamie had been going on, his dad would be spending pounds on expensive presents, so theirs would be completely insignificant.

Meanwhile, John was busy with scissors, glue and plastic sheeting. He had remembered that Jamie hadn't had a pencil case, or probably just forgotten to bring it, but Mum always said it was the thought that counted. John had decided to make him a case with special sections for pens, pencils, ruler and dinner money. The money section didn't turn out quite right because he really needed a press stud but the rest fitted together very cleverly.

Mum found some new pencils and a few coloured crayons left over from the twins' party and John pushed these into the right compartments. All in all, it looked fine. The twins wrapped up their evening's efforts in some brightly coloured paper, printed Jamie's name and left the parcel on the kitchen table overnight.

'It isn't much, just something John made but anyway, Happy Birthday from us both,' Sarah said at break-time the next day. She shoved the present awkwardly into Jamie's hand.

He hadn't said a word about his birthday all morning – in fact the twins had started to think they'd misheard him the previous evening, but then Mrs Lucas had mentioned it during register time. She'd even let Jamie measure the water in the rain-catching tube which was a real privilege, because of his birthday, but he hadn't seemed very pleased.

Now, he took the parcel as if it might be a bomb

and stared at the twins unbelievingly.

'For me?' he asked.

'Why don't you open it?' Sarah said a bit roughly, to cover her embarrassment. She could imagine Jamie's scornful look when he saw it was just something home-made. If only John hadn't come up with such a daft idea.

Jamie fumbled with the sellotape, like he was afraid of tearing the paper, until the present was revealed. It looked even smaller now and the writing on the card, Sarah noticed, was a bit wonky. The twins were amazed at Jamie's delight.

'Hey, that's great!' he said and his mouth really *did* manage a smile this time. 'Did you make it?'

'Oh yes, it didn't take long,' John boasted.

'I did the card,' Sarah said, anxious to take some credit now that Jamie was enthusiastic.

'It's really nice, er . . . thanks.' He said it awkwardly, but they could tell Jamie was pleased and that made them both feel really good inside.

Sarah wondered if Jamie was just being polite but he kept the pencil case and the card on his desk all day, as if it was the best thing he'd had for weeks. The twins felt a bit more encouraged. Teatime might be OK at this rate. For the rest of the day Jamie seemed almost happy and even helped Sarah do some more lettering for the coastguard project. He still didn't say a word about his birthday presents but John supposed he wanted to surprise them when they got to his home. John hoped there were some decent games to play with, or a model he could help Jamie start. Sarah just hoped they wouldn't have trifle for tea, because she hated it.

56

People were always having trifle at parties and Mum said it wasn't polite not to eat a little if it was offered.

At last, the afternoon bell rang and everyone packed up. The twins waited for Jamie to pack up but he took ages. He didn't seem in any hurry to go home, and the cheerful look on his face had gone again. They waited in the playground for Mrs Clark to arrive.

'Will we meet your dad?' Sarah asked, just for something to say.

'No,' Jamie replied, very sharply. 'He's got to work late.'

'Oh, that's a shame.'

'He's got a really important job, so no one else can help him, see.'

'Well, what did you get for your birthday, then?' John asked, his curiosity getting the better of him.

'Oh, I got a bike.'

'Great, I've got one,' John said.

'Mine's a racing bike, with ten gears.'

'Ten! Crikey, that sounds fantastic. Do you reckon I can have a go?'

'Oh, I don't know. It's in the garage, see, and Dad wanted to check it over before I ride it.'

'Did he get it from the newspaper? That's where mine came from.'

'No, it's brand new. It's still got the paper on – I haven't had time to look at it properly yet.'

'Still, we can see it, can't we?'

'Yeah, maybe, I'll see.'

Throughout the conversation, Jamie's eyes flicked around and he kept kicking his toe into the gravel, making little stones jump up.

'There's my mum,' he said quickly, before John could ask any more questions.

It was a rather awkward drive home. Mrs Clark asked the twins lots of questions about their home, parents and hobbies. She seemed to be trying very hard to make them feel welcome but Jamie, sitting in the front of the car, was gloomy and silent. He really was an odd kid, Sarah thought.

Jamie's house was at the end of a line of small, newish buildings with tiny front gardens. Opposite, there was a garage block and spaces for cars to park. Mrs Clark took a basket of shopping out of the boot and then led the children across the road and into the house. A smell of cake wafted out to meet them.

While Mrs Clark made some drinks Jamie showed them into the lounge. The twins were always fascinated by new places and their eyes were everywhere taking in the details of the room. The furniture was all quite big, and didn't seem to fit in the small room. A small portable TV was balanced on the edge of a shelf. There was no sign of a video or the expensive hi-fi equipment. Perhaps it was in another room, John thought. The dining table was set for tea, with bright red plates and lots of different kinds of sandwiches under cling-film.

'Can we see your cards?' Sarah said politely.

'Yeah, if you like,' Jamie replied.

There were lots of cards, most of them on the shelf over the gas fire. John fingered them lightly as he turned each one over. There were messages from various aunts and uncles but when John looked at the card which had 'To a dear son' written

58

on the front, he couldn't help noticing that it was only signed 'love, Mum'. He looked around casually for any other cards but there weren't any, and just then Mrs Clark came in with a tray of drinks.

'Why don't you play in the garden before tea?' she suggested. 'You can get out the swingball.'

It wasn't a very good game for three people but the twins said they'd like to play – anything was better than just sitting around.

'Cor, your grass needs cutting,' John remarked. The back lawn was about eight inches high.

'It was like that when we moved in and Mum hasn't had a chance to cut it yet,' Jamie explained.

'Dad always does the lawns, but I help him sometimes,' John said.

Jamie swung at the ball viciously and Sarah had to duck as it almost hit her ear. After that, she handed her bat to John and sat down to watch. It seemed that Jamie didn't really like them being here at all. If only it was time to go.

At last it was tea-time. They filed back inside, washed their hands and sat down to tea. Nobody seemed to be very hungry although the food was nice. John and Sarah ate away steadily but the piles of sandwiches still looked huge when they had to admit to being full up. Neither Jamie or his mum had managed to finish more than one each. There were some chocolate and peppermint slices to follow, nut biscuits and birthday cake. Sarah was glad they didn't have to sing Happy Birthday. She felt too old for that now. Also, it wouldn't be much fun to sing Happy Birthday to someone looking as miserable as Jamie did. She wished John wouldn't keep kicking her under the table. It was very irritating. Sarah frowned across at him to stop but he was blinking at her like he did when he wanted to attract her attention. What on earth was he up to now?

'Have you had quite enough to eat?'

'Yes, thank you Mrs Clark,' Sarah replied, ignoring John, who was blinking away like mad.

'Well, perhaps you'd like to see Jamie's presents. Go and show them, love,' she said to Jamie.

'Oh, out in the garage you mean?' John said, getting up excitedly.

Mrs Clark looked surprised and Jamie blushed a deep red.

'No, up in my bedroom,' he said. 'Come on.'

The twins exchanged glances and then followed him.

'Can't we see your bike?' John asked when they were all sitting on Jamie's bed upstairs, looking at some new books he'd had.

'No, it's had to go back to the shop – there was something wrong with it. Some of the paint was scratched and Dad said it was going to have to go back.'

'Which shop did you get it from?'

'I don't know!' Jamie snapped back.

'Sorry, I just wondered,' John said a bit indignantly.

Sarah gazed at Jamie and frowned. A little while ago he'd said the bike was still wrapped up – now it was scratched. It didn't make sense.

'I'm going to the bathroom,' Jamie said, getting up. He thrust his hands into his pockets and stamped out of the room. The door clicked shut behind him. The twins looked at each other, not quite sure what to say.

'He's weird!' Sarah finally announced.

'There's something funny going on,' John agreed.

'What was all that about the bike?'

'Who knows? I'm more interested in the birthday card.'

'Pardon?'

'I'm almost sure there isn't one from his dad. It was only signed from his mum.'

'Well, that doesn't mean anything – he might have got a separate card from his dad and it's been put up somewhere else.'

'I didn't see it,' John argued.

'That's daft. He couldn't be lying. I mean, he wouldn't do a thing like that . . .' Sarah trailed off a bit uncertainly.

One of the things she and John had always been taught was that you shouldn't tell lies. They thought that everyone told the truth.

'We must just have heard wrong,' she said.

'But we didn't! He told us lots of things about his dad, but they don't make any sense. Haven't you noticed something about this house – there aren't any things in it which belong to his dad!'

'What do you mean?'

'Have you seen any shoes, or coats or books that could belong to his dad? There aren't any of those things.'

'Oh, John!' Sarah felt excited and at the same time a bit afraid. Was there really some awful secret being kept from them or had they made a daft mistake?

'What about Mrs Clark? She's too nice and ordinary to be telling lies.'

'But she hasn't, don't you see?'

'No, I don't see,' Sarah said, rubbing her forehead.

'Well, *she* hasn't talked about her husband or the bike or anything. . . . It's only Jamie who's been telling us about them.'

'And when you said about going to the garage, he looked really guilty,' Sarah remembered.

'Exactly!'

'But, if he's really making it all up, why is he doing it?'

'That's what we've got to find out!' John exclaimed. 'It's our next mystery to solve.'

'We haven't solved the last one yet,' Sarah reminded him.

'Yes, well, maybe we can sort Mr Linden out when we get to the bottom of the Jamie Clark case.'

Sarah bit her lip thoughtfully. Apart from asking Jamie straight, she didn't know how they could prove whether what he was saying was true or not.

They heard steps on the landing and picked up a book each, pretending to be reading it. They mustn't look as if they'd been talking about him or he'd know they were on to him. Jamie stood in the doorway sulkily and rubbed the back of his leg with one foot.

'What do you want to do?' he asked, not looking up.

'Have you got any games?' Sarah asked.

He went across to a cupboard and took out some boxes of games that looked ages old. Sarah took one that she liked and started setting out the board and the pieces. It was a battery-operated board with plastic fish which opened and shut their mouths at intervals as the inside of the board turned round. Each player had a fishing rod, with a hook on the end. If you had a steady hand and were quick enough, you could catch the fish by flicking it out of the pond. Generally, you were too slow though and the mouth closed before there was time to hook it.

Jamie just watched for a while as Sarah and John crouched over the board trying to outdo each other in skill and speed. At last, his sense of competition got the better of his bad mood so he grabbed a rod and joined in. It became a fast frustrating match especially as they ran out of fish near the end and everyone was trying to hook the last two. John got one and then Jamie got the other. It meant that he had just won. They played several more games until Mrs Clark came upstairs with some more squash and also to find out why there was so much noise. She wasn't at all worried about it, though – in fact she kept on smiling and saying how glad she was that the twins had been able to come.

Jamie was good fun too, when he was really concentrating on the game. It was as if he had forgotten whatever had made him angry. John wished he knew what it was.

At last, Mrs Clark said that it was nearly time for Mr Ward to arrive so they ought to be packing up. Sarah was quite sorry, but as they put the board back in its box John started asking questions again.

'Are you coming to church on Sunday?'

'I suppose I'll have to,' Jamie scowled.

'Don't you like it then?'

'I hate it.'

'Why do you come, then?' Sarah interrupted.

'Cos Mum does.'

'And your dad?'

'No, he stays at home.'

'Couldn't you stay with him then?'

'I suppose so . . .' Jamie's voice trailed off and then, to the twins' horror, his eyes sort of filled up and he put his head down. He brushed his nose with his sleeve roughly and made a loud snuffly, choking noise.

'Are you all right?' Sarah asked.

'Course I am!' he returned crossly.

There was a horrible silence and no-one knew quite what to say. The doorbell rang. Thank goodness, Sarah sighed. It had to be their dad. She got to her feet and sidled towards the door.

'Well thanks, Jamie,' Sarah said awkwardly.

'It's OK,' he muttered.

Mrs Clark was chatting to their dad as the twins trotted down the stairs with Jamie behind them.

'Hello, you two – had a nice time?' Mr Ward smiled.

Sarah stood next to him, liking the office smell of pens and photocopying which clung to his work suit. 'Yes, thanks,' she said politely.

'And this is Jamie. Hello, young man – had a good day?'

Jamie nodded shyly.

Sarah thought they were just going to say good-bye, give their thank-yous and go home but John had worked out a clever detective plan. It was just a simple sentence but the effect was very surprising.

'Thanks, Jamie, I hope your dad gets the bike back for you soon. I can't wait to see it.'

Mrs Clark looked as if she was going to faint. Her face went white and she suddenly gripped Jamie by the shoulder with her hand.

'Jamie!' she said, terribly quietly. 'What on earth have you been saying?'

Jamie looked so guilty and wretched that Sarah felt really sorry for him. He squirmed to get his shoulder free but Mrs Clark held on even harder.

'What's all this about a bike?' she demanded, shaking him a little.

Something seemed to snap in Jamie. 'I didn't get a bike for my birthday!' he flared, staring at the twins. 'I didn't get *anything* from my dad ... because he's in prison.'

He wrenched himself free and charged up the stairs, slamming his bedroom door behind him. Mrs Clark held on to the bannister and tried to give a smile which didn't come out.

'I'm so sorry, he's very upset about it all. . . .'

The twins stood wide-eyed, horrified. John could hardly believe his ears.

'Children, go and sit in the car, please', Mr Ward said, taking charge. They went.

John and Sarah sat in the back of the car and waited. Across the road, they could see their dad talking to Mrs Clark. She was running her hand through her hair and nodding her head a lot.

'Well, that's that!' Sarah said. 'Jamie will never talk to us again.'

'So what! He spun a whole load of lies to us. I don't care if we never see him again.'

The adults were shaking hands now, then they saw their father's tall figure striding towards the car. He didn't say very much and, although the twins were dying to find out what Mrs Clark had said, they didn't dare ask.

Back at home they were sent upstairs to have their baths earlier than usual and Sarah guessed that their parents were discussing Jamie in the kitchen downstairs.

'I bet Mum'll say we can't ever see Jamie again, anyway,' John said, as he rubbed his short hair on the towel, outside Sarah's bedroom. He sounded quite pleased.

'Why?' Sarah was concentrating on getting the tangles out of her hair. 'Because his dad's in prison, you mean?'

'Well, no.' John supposed you couldn't help it if your dad was in prison but if *you* were a liar and made up daft stories that was something else.

'I don't suppose he's told us one thing about himself that's true,' John decided, 'and we even fell for it at first!' He was thoroughly pleased that he'd got to the bottom of Jamie's 'problem' but Sarah couldn't stop thinking of Jamie's face just before he'd turned away.

'Perhaps *we'd* lie, if our dad was in prison,' she suggested.

'Never – it's wrong and it's cowardly. Well, it is about big things like that,' John added, remembering one or two tiny lies he'd told.

'Maybe it doesn't matter whether they're big or little – to God I mean.'

John didn't answer. He was convinced. They'd never liked Jamie – now they had all the reason they needed not to bother with him any more. That made the conversation with their mum and dad at supper-time very hard to understand, especially when Dad's first words were, 'We want you to invite Jamie back to tea as soon as possible.'

Chapter Five

'No way!' John cried, his cheeks getting red with indignation.

'Now, listen,' Dad said calmly. 'Jamie hasn't done anything to hurt you. It only needs both of you to try to understand him and he could be a really good friend.'

'Who'd want a friend like that? You can't trust him and you'd never know when he was telling the truth.'

'That's missing the point,' Dad said.

'But *we* get told off when we tell lies,' Sarah put in, feeling that she had to back John up on this one. It was typical of adults to have one rule for you and quite different ones for themselves or everyone else.

'I know it is wrong to tell lies,' Dad agreed, 'but can't we also remember how important it is to forgive people?'

Sarah screwed her nose up. She was thinking of last Sunday when Jamie had got her into trouble. She'd been told to forgive him then, and she *had*. Fat lot of good it had done. Jamie hadn't changed at all. He'd just thought of a massive big story to fool them with.

Mum had been doing the ironing quietly but she set the iron down while she fetched some more water. Clouds of hissing steam shot out angrily when the water chamber was full again. She tested it on the cover before sweeping across the hem of Sarah's best dress. Sarah watched the creases disappear as the iron cut a path over the material. Mum kept going across the same piece as if she wasn't really attending to the job.

'What do you say, Mum?' John asked, appealing to her.

'Your dad's right, John.'

'Huh!' John put his chin in his hand moodily. Grown-ups always stuck together. It was only because they were afraid of losing an argument.

'I don't see why I have to forgive Jamie,' John declared mutinously.

'Nor do I,' said Sarah, 'because I already *have* and it hasn't made any difference, so I won't again.'

'Do you know how many times Jesus told his disciples they had to forgive someone?' Mum asked.

John thought, but he didn't know. He shook his head.

'Seventy times seven!'

'What!' Sarah exclaimed.

'That's daft,' John declared. 'Who'd do that!'

'That's what the Bible says. And I don't think

Jesus meant exactly that number of times anyway. I think he probably meant there was no limit to the number of times we should be prepared to forgive each other.'

'Infinity times!' John said. They'd been doing infinity numbers at school. It was fascinating, because it meant you could never get to the end of them, and he just liked saying the word and imagining lines of numbers going on for ever.

'Think about it son,' Dad said. 'How many times have you done handstands against your bedroom wall and got dirty footmarks on the paintwork?'

John didn't suppose it was quite up to seventy times seven yet but it might be getting on that way.

'A few times,' he admitted.

'And in spite of me having a fit each time I catch you, does it stop you?'

John grinned.

'But what if I *refused* to forgive you for doing it? That would be silly, because we'd never be friends again. In fact though, I do keep forgiving you, and you even forgive me for not letting you stay up to watch TV after nine o'clock.'

John laughed. He knew what his dad meant. Sometimes, when he was sent off to bed he stormed out of the room saying he didn't love his dad any more. Once in bed though, he always regretted it. Well, it was just words you said when you were cross and upset.

'Jamie forgives his father too,' Dad added, more seriously now. 'He feels really let down, because his dad stole some money from his business. That means he has to serve a prison sentence. But Jamie loves his dad, so he tries to pretend that he's one of the best dads in the world. That's what all the lies were about.'

'So it doesn't matter if he lies?' Sarah asked.

'Yes, it does, love, but if you can understand *why* he does it, perhaps we can all help him not to do it. He probably thinks no-one will like him with a dad in prison, so that's another reason. And maybe he feels cross with his dad as well, for leaving him and his mum.'

'Is that why they've moved houses?'

'Yes, partly. They couldn't afford to live in their old house and Mrs Clark wanted Jamie to have a new start because some of his friends had been a bit mean to him.'

Sarah was sympathetic at once. 'How horrible! That's really unkind,' she cried, immediately on Jamie's side.

John was beginning to soften but he still felt a bit suspicious.

'It's nearly time for bed,' Mum said. 'Why don't you go and get ready, both of you, and I'll be up to tell you a story as soon as I've finished here.'

The twins shot off at once. Now that they both read quite well themselves it was a treat for Mum to read *to* them. When they were settled on Sarah's bed as usual, Mum came in, not with a story book but with John's Bible. She sat down between them and put her arms round their shoulders comfortably.

'You can't hold the book, Mum, like this,' John pointed out.

'It's OK. I know this story very well.'

'What's it about, then?'

'Two brothers, and their father.'

'Right, go on then,' John encouraged.

'Well, this man had two sons who worked on the family farm.'

'Did they have cows?' Sarah interrupted.

'Yes, they had cows and goats and they grew some crops as well. One day, the younger boy decided he'd like to travel around the world, so he asked his dad to give him a large sum of money. The father was rather upset but he loved the boy, so he said, "Yes, all right," and the boy took his money and left.'

'What about the older brother?'

'He stayed at home with his dad and helped to run the farm.'

'So the man wasn't lonely then?' Sarah asked.

'Well, yes, he was really, because although he'd got his first boy, he loved his other boy so much that he missed him, and worried about him. In fact, he used to go out looking for him every day, just in case he was coming home.'

'Meanwhile the boy had a great time at first, spending money travelling, meeting new people. But he never met any good friends. They just used his money and then, when it was all gone, they wouldn't speak to him. So eventually he was so poor he had to eat scraps that people put out for their animals. He was alone, hungry and very miserable. He decided to go home. On the way home he was very ashamed, and afraid that his dad wouldn't want him any more.'

'Oh, but he did, didn't he!' Sarah put in.

'Of course he did. When he saw the boy, he rushed out of the gates to welcome him, and he hugged him tight and gave him new clothes and a very expensive ring. Then he said that they were all going to have a party to celebrate the boy coming home.'

'Wasn't he cross about the money?'

'He was upset that the boy had been foolish, but he forgave him.'

'So everyone lived happily ever after?'

'Well, in the Bible story there's just one problem. What do you think the older brother felt like when the young boy came home?'

John and Sarah thought hard. 'Was he expecting his dad to tell him off for wasting the money?' John said.

'Yes, he was.'

'It was a bit unfair on him I suppose,' Sarah said.

'That's what he thought, so he told his dad so.'

'What did his dad say?'

'His dad told him that he loved both of his sons very much and even though the young one had been silly he wasn't going to punish him.'

'I expect he wished he hadn't wasted the money anyway,' Sarah put in.

'I'm sure he did.'

'Did they all live happily?'

'It doesn't say in the Bible.'

'I think the older boy understood and forgave his younger brother when he'd had time to think about it,' Sarah announced.

John was silent.

Mum kissed them both and tucked Sarah in while

John made his way back to his own room. He was thinking hard when she came to tuck him in.

'Everyone deserves a second chance if they make a mistake, don't they?' he said.

'Yes,' Mum agreed, 'I think they do.'

'Can Jamie come to tea on Friday?' he said, unexpectedly.

'Of course. Ask him tomorrow.'

John was asleep almost before Mum had picked up his clothes and tidied some books on his desk.

At school the next day, the twins began to realise that making friends with people wasn't just a one-way thing. They treated Jamie as nicely as they could, without overdoing it, but he seemed determined to ignore them. At first John couldn't understand it but as he watched Jamie mooching around on his own at dinner time, he realised how foolish Jamie must be feeling.

'We've got to do something to make him realise we're not just feeling sorry for him,' John told Sarah.

'I suppose so, but I can't think how.'

'We could ask for his help on something.'

'Like what?'

'I don't know. Anything.'

'Well, he isn't very good at helping,' Sarah pointed out.

'That's only because he isn't interested in school things.'

'How can we cheer him up then? Did you ask him to tea?'

'Yes, but he said something about being too

busy. I know he just doesn't want to come to our house and I don't really blame him. You know how he'd feel.'

It seemed an impossible problem but in the end, the twins discovered that Jamie could help them in a very exciting way, and it was all because of the project.

Everyone else had been busy working away on their topics all week, but although it had seemed such a brilliant idea, John and Sarah still couldn't find out much about the coastguards. As a result they only had a few measly pictures and one map to put in their project folder. There was no way they were going to win the prize. They had even thought about changing the subject when, on Friday during topic time, Jamie came up with a brilliant suggestion.

'You know I couldn't come to tea tonight?' he said very casually.

'Yes.'

'Well, it's because my uncle is coming to stay the weekend. He's my mum's younger brother and he's a sailor.'

'Really?' John enthused.

'Yeah, well I asked him on the phone last night about your project and he thinks he can get you an invite to look round Berryman Coastguard Centre. He's done a Coastguard course in Bournemouth, you see, and he thinks he knows one of the blokes who works there.'

'Brilliant! That's fantastic!' John shouted, making the teacher turn round and stare at them.

'When can we go?'

'I'm not sure,' Jamie said. 'Look, I don't want you to be disappointed, I mean, he said it was pretty likely but I can't promise . . . you know.'

The twins understood exactly. Jamie had tried to do something good for them as a way of making up, and he didn't want this to go wrong, like it all had before.

'It's really nice of you, Jamie,' Sarah said.

He shrugged, a bit embarrassed. 'Well, it'll help with your project.'

'It's *our* project,' John reminded him firmly.

'Right then, give us that bit of paper and I'll start writing down some questions we want to have answered,' Jamie volunteered, his eyes bright.

'Great! It'll be a kind of interview,' Sarah said, 'and we can write it out like a newspaper.'

The twins never doubted that Jamie's uncle would be able to fix the trip and while they were eating tea at home, Mrs Clark phoned to arrange the visit for Saturday afternoon. The time between was endless, as far as the twins were concerned. They were determined to make it a really professional interview and Sarah practised most of Saturday morning, asking her mum questions and then scribbling down the answers in her own system of shorthand. She decided that after being a policewoman and a nurse she could enjoy being a journalist.

The twins spent some time in the tree house during the morning and the sight of Mr Linden's identikit picture jogged their memories.

'We still haven't worked out what he was digging up, or what his mysterious parcel contained,' Sarah said.

'Ah well, we got diverted onto another case,' John reminded her. 'We've solved the Jamie Clark case so now we can return to "Operation Linden".'

'We haven't seen him for days.'

'That doesn't matter. He probably thinks he's safe to move now, but we'll be ready for him. When we get back this evening we'll spend at least two hours keeping his house under surveillance.'

'What's surveillance?' Sarah asked.

'It means you watch someone.'

'Well, why didn't you say so?'

'Because surveillance is the proper word. You've got to learn the proper police words for when we join the force,' John insisted.

'I might be a journalist,' Sarah replied, flicking her notebook in a very dramatic way.

Girls! John thought. They were always changing their minds! He didn't say this aloud, though.

'I can hear a car!' Sarah cried, scrambling down the ladder backwards.

'We'll be back,' John murmured, with just a quick backward glance at Mr Linden's poster, as he followed his sister.

Jamie's Uncle Chris was talking to their parents when the twins reached the house. Sarah was a bit shy at first but, in the end, it was decided that Dad was going to come with them so everything was perfect, even though it meant squeezing into the back seat with John and Jamie leaping around like a couple of baboons.

'John, you're sitting on me!' Sarah cried, digging him with an elbow.

78

Jamie's uncle was such good fun that they soon forgot how squashed they were. He drove over every bump in the road, so that they were jolted all over the place, and told them jokes which were pathetic but still made them laugh. Sarah was quite glad when the journey ended though, because she was beginning to feel a bit sick.

'Now, if I introduce you three,' Chris said, 'I think it'd be best if your dad and I stayed back. There's not a lot of room in the station anyway, and as it's your project, I think you ought to do it in your own way.'

Dad agreed so he sat in the car while Chris ushered them into the white building. Their first impression was how cramped and untidy everything seemed. There was a tiny area with a sink and some mugs in one corner. Then they went through into the main office. Here they were met by Jim Tucker, the most senior coastguard on duty. He had his sleeves rolled up and looked busy scribbling away at some papers, but he stood up when they entered and shook hands firmly with all four.

'So you're my special visitors!' he boomed. The man had a deep, large voice and his face was red and smiling. He had thick white eyebrows which nearly met in the middle. The top of his head was bald and he kept smoothing the deep brown skin there with his hand as he talked.

Sarah liked him, but she felt so shy she was sure she wouldn't be able to ask a single question. Chris exchanged a few words with Jim and then left them to it. The boys were already standing wide-eyed in front of a screen which had dots blipping across it.

They had no idea what the dots were supposed to be.

Another man, a bit younger than Jim, sat at the opposite desk. He had a pair of earphones on and was writing something down.

Jim consulted his watch. 'You're just in time,' he said, winking. 'I'm a radio star too, you know! Listen to this.'

Jim picked up a phone and at the same time tuned in a small radio to the frequency of the local radio station, Westair. It was the usual Saturday afternoon show – some music, sports news and leisure pursuits spot.

'I have ninety seconds just after the news to give a local shipping report,' Jim explained. He flicked a switch and the children could hear him talking to the DJ by phone. On the radio, a record was being played. As it finished the two o'clock news came on, then the DJ introduced Jim Tucker and Jim gave his forecast. It was apparently fair for all water sports but freshening winds were expected later on, so surfers should be careful. The boys were fascinated as they heard Jim's booming voice relayed back to them in the next room on the radio. Sarah started scribbling notes in her pad. This was going to make fantastic stuff for their project. They'd never realised this was a part of a coastguard's job.

Once the radio slot was finished, Jim took them on a tour of the building. He was full of stories about people or animals that they'd helped to rescue. He let them touch the equipment and John even took an incoming call from a ship which wanted to check its position. John was glad to pass the headset over to Jim, though, for the answer. The responsibility of making sure ships didn't collide seemed enormous.

Eventually Sarah managed to ask some of her questions and she was scribbling away like fury trying to get down all the important bits of information Jim had for her.

They went outside to look at the aerials and then inside to see how each aerial was linked to a telephone.

'Usually we have two men manning the phones at any one time but the office next door has three more lines so we can call in extra men if there are more calls than usual. We aim to answer any call for help in six minutes. The distress channel, channel 16, is manned twenty-four hours a day.'

'How can you hear what they say with all the interferences?' Jamie asked.

'Well, it's difficult,' Jim admitted. 'The trouble is that three aerials produce a lot of what we call static fuzz. Sometimes they block each other out. You have to concentrate very hard at all times.'

'What if you missed a call?' John asked.

'We haven't yet, but there is a possibility – we can't deny that.'

'Why don't you have more men?'

'Money!' Jim sighed. 'We actually have to rely a lot on volunteers as it is.'

'I wish I could be a volunteer,' Jamie said.

'Well, maybe one day! We're always on the look-out for dedicated men and women who can react quickly and calmly in times of crisis.'

'Are all coastguard stations on cliffs?' John asked.

'No, lad, not these days. You see, we have equipment which can pick up signals from ships without us needing to see the ships themselves. Mind you, we still have our telescope up here. The cliffs around can be fairly dangerous and it doesn't do any harm to keep an eye out every so often. Come on and I'll show you.'

The three children followed him to the front window of the building where a telescope on a swivel was mounted, like the ones on the seafront where you put ten pence in for a few minutes view.

'You may have to focus a bit,' Jim explained as each in turn pressed their eyes to the telescope.

'I'll just leave you here for a moment,' Jim said, slipping back to his desk.

The children focused on huge tankers sailing far out on the horizon where they looked like black monsters, slicing through the water.

'I'm going to focus on the cliffs,' John said, sliding the instrument round and down to the headland where they'd walked last weekend.

What he saw after a few moments made his knuckles whiten on the metal case.

'Sarah,' he whispered, not daring to move his head in case he lost the image.

'What?'

'It's him! He's down there!'

'Who?' Sarah said, whispering as well even though she didn't know why.

'Mr Linden!'

Chapter Six

'Who?' Jamie asked, pushing John out of the way.

'Don't! I'll lose him,' John cried, fending him off, and trying to keep his eyes on the lenses at the same time.

'Well now,' Jim boomed, returning to the look-out position, 'if you've finished here I'll let you see the emergency procedures before you go.'

'Thank you,' Sarah said, dragging her brother away from the telescope where he and Jamie were still jostling.

'Come on, John!' she hissed.

'Spotted anything, lad?' Jim asked.

'What? Oh, er, no, nothing really,' John stammered.

Jamie kept nudging John trying to find out what he was making all the fuss about but Sarah had got hold of the sleeve of John's jumper and wouldn't let go.

The coastguard had opened a crate containing thick metal-covered cylinders.

'These are flares,' he explained.

'I thought the people in the boats had them,' Sarah said.

'Well, yes, they should always carry flares, in case their radios fail, but we use them here to alert the lifeboat crew.'

Sarah looked puzzled.

'These flares are visible for several miles once they go up, and there's a powerful explosive charge which makes a pretty loud noise. The men from the lifeboat carry walkie-talkies but the flares act as a warning too. They can reach the quay, just down the coast there, and be on the lifeboat in seven minutes – not bad, eh?'

The three children fingered the flares carefully. They were heavy and solid to touch.

'Could we send one up?' Jamie wanted to know.

' 'Fraid not, lad,' Jim smiled. 'These are expensive and in any case, they're strictly for emergency use.'

He looked at his watch. 'I think it's about time I did some work so I'll have to let you three go. But first let me give you some leaflets which you might find interesting. Have you heard of our "Don't sink the Coastguard Campaign"?'

'Was there something about it on TV?' Sarah said.

'That's right, lass. There's quite a lot of local support, being a busy fishing and tourist community, you see. There are plans to close a lot of stations like this one and centralise operations. That means there'd be fewer stations with better equipment, but you know what we'd lose?'

'Er, no,' Sarah said, struggling for an answer.

'Local knowledge, my dear!' Jim announced triumphantly.

'Oh, I see,' Sarah said, not quite sure that she did.

'When it comes to rescuing people, or animals come to that, there's nothing so good as first-hand knowledge – people who know where the coastal paths run and where the dangerous bits are. If you're fifty miles away you can't know that, can you?'

'No,' Sarah agreed quickly. Jim looked as if he was going to get really wound up about the subject and in fact they'd already been here an hour so she tried to edge towards the door without looking impolite.

'You've been ever so kind, sir,' Sarah thanked him. She gave John and Jamie a meaningful stare and they quickly gave their thanks as well.

'It's been a pleasure, my dears. When you've finished your project, perhaps you'll let me see it.'

'Oh yes, of course,' they chorused.

'And remember – your coastguards are the friends of all sea and coast users, and people didn't ought to forget that.'

'I'm sure they won't,' Jamie said soothingly.

'Goodbye, sir,' Sarah said, holding out her hand.

'Goodbye, lass,' Jim replied, enclosing her entire hand in his great strong one.

The next minute, they were out in the fresh air, shivering a little in the stiffening breeze.

'His forecast was correct,' Jamie said, flapping his arms around his chest to keep warm.

'Honestly, John, you were a real show-up,' Sarah scolded, putting on her teacher's voice. When there was no reply she glanced round to see John haring off towards the cliff path.

'John! Come back!' she shouted crossly.

'Where's he off to?' Jamie said, standing with his arms akimbo.

'Another of his stupid detective games,' Sarah said, rather scornfully. She forgot that up until quite recently, she'd been just as keen on the idea as John.

'Detective game? What *are* you going on about?'

Sarah blushed. It suddenly dawned on her that telling Jamie that they were on the path of a criminal wasn't quite tactful, in view of the fact that his own dad was in prison. Why didn't John come back? She shaded her eyes with one hand and scanned the distance where John's fair head could be seen bobbing up and down between the gorse bushes.

'Oh, well, if it's some great secret!' Jamie said crossly.

'It's not that . . . well, it's just a game really. John'll tell you about it when he comes back.'

'Huh! I don't care, I don't want to know anyway.'

Sarah was torn. It had been just between John and her. They didn't share this game with anyone. But then she thought of the great time they'd had with the coastguard. Her pad was full of notes and she held a wad of pamphlets in her hand. Jamie had given them this adventure so it was only fair to share at least a bit of the secret. John couldn't complain anyway because if he hadn't acted so stupidly in the coastguards' office no-one would have said anything. Jamie had walked away from her and turned his back. Sarah decided that it wasn't enough just to be nice to him; that wasn't really being a friend, not in the proper sense. Being a real friend meant treating people exactly as you would want them to treat you. It wasn't nice to be left out of things. Sarah walked over to Jamie and punched his arm roughly.

'Can you keep a secret?' she challenged.

'Course I can!' Jamie said, running a finger across his throat, just to prove it.

'Well then, listen . . .' and Sarah quickly told him their suspicions about Mr Linden. When she'd finished, Jamie looked a bit doubtful.

'Doesn't sound like much of a mystery to me,' he said. 'Anyway, what's John doing now?'

'Following him, I expect.'

'You mean he's *here* right this minute?'

'Yes, that's what John was trying to tell me in the coastguard station.'

'Well, let's get after him, then!'

'We can't, your uncle will be back in a minute, in fact I can see them coming now.'

'No problem, they're busy talking. I'll tell Uncle Chris we're just making a plan of the coastline here. You go and catch up with John, then wait for me.'

Sarah hesitated for just a minute and then took off after John. The wind whipped through her hair and made her eyes sting. It was difficult running downhill and she could feel the stones on the track jabbing through the soles of her trainers. Sarah was pelting along so fast that she nearly went flying headfirst as the path become more uneven. She steadied herself and started to look around. More by luck than anything else she suddenly spotted John just below her, edging along behind some bushes. He glanced over his shoulder and saw Sarah just in time to stop her from shouting out.

'What are you doing?' she whispered as she dropped down beside him onto her knees.

'Mr Linden is just over the next ridge. We've got to see what he's up to. The plan is, we climb down a bit and then creep up on him, just so we can get a closer look.'

'We've got to wait for Jamie,' Sarah said.

'What! You've told *him*! Oh honestly, Sarah.'

'Don't go on at me. It was your fault. . . .'

'Keep your voice down, Sarah,' John warned, interrupting her. 'All right, then, wait here for Jamie, then circle round to that spot – but you *must* keep down.'

'OK.'

Sarah waited, crouched down until she was getting stiff. John was out of sight and she couldn't hear Jamie's footsteps yet. The wind, which was getting stronger, howled in her ears. Sarah put up the hood of her anorak and waited.

At last Jamie reached her. She told him to follow her and for once he didn't argue. They half ran, half crawled to the position John had described. It was quite a way from the path and Sarah felt a bit scared. She knew they shouldn't really be off the track. But then both children caught sight of John and, more excitingly, Mr Linden. Even Jamie gasped. There was no way Mr Linden could be just another afternoon walker. He was walking away from them towards some evil-looking rocks. He was dressed for climbing with a rope slung around his waist, knee length trousers and heavy boots. He had a short-handled spade in one hand and a sack in the other. The sack looked heavy, as if it was sagging under some weight inside it and there was no doubt that Mr Linden was being very secretive. Every few steps he took, he looked back over his shoulder. The children couldn't see much of his face because the cap was pulled way down over his eyes, but the beard was unmistakable. From their two vantage places the children watched his movements for several minutes before he disappeared way below them and out of sight.

'Did he know we were following him?' Jamie asked, breaking the silence.

'I don't think so, we kept out of sight.'

'Well, he must have thought *someone* was following,' Sarah suggested. She stood up and beckoned to John who was climbing back towards them. His face was red with the effort and also through excitement.

'What do you think *now*, then?' he exclaimed triumphantly.

Sarah shrugged her shoulders, but she had to admit that this time there was definitely something odd about their neighbour. Adults could be pretty stupid at times, but this wasn't normal behaviour.

'How long have you known about him, then?' Jamie wanted to know.

'Oh, we've had him under observation for some time now,' John replied rather grandly.

'Really! Well, that's great. Hey, I don't suppose you'll let me join you would you, as part of the detective team?'

'Well, I don't know. How much training have you had?'

Jamie thought. 'Well, I've been in court once.'

'Have you really?' John said, impressed.

'Well, outside of one actually,' Jamie admitted.

It was still more than John and Sarah had done. 'Well, I suppose we could do with another man on the job.'

'I think we ought to tell Dad,' Sarah announced.

John stared at her as if she was mad.

'Well,' Sarah defended herself, 'he might be up to no good at all. We don't know what he was burying. . . .'

'Or digging up!' Jamie suggested.

'Well, whatever,' Sarah argued, 'I still think we should tell Dad.'

'He'd do absolutely nothing,' John said. 'For a start we still don't know what was in the sack, and you can't go telling Dad there was a man with a sack. I mean, that's not exactly against the law or anything. He'd just say "Oh, that's interesting," or something and forget all about it. No, we've got to watch him closer than ever until we've got some solid facts.'

'You *are* lucky, living right next door to him,' Jamie said, rather sadly.

'Hey, why don't you stay the night?' Sarah said. 'There's a spare bed in John's room.'

'Yeah, we'll ask Dad,' John said. 'Come on. Let's go.'

'Well, you're back at last!' Uncle Chris said. 'We were about to send out the search party.'

'How was the coastguard station, then?' Dad asked, ruffling John's hair as he climbed into the car.

'Great,' John said.

'Tell us all about it then.'

John kept up a commentary for several minutes, with help from Jamie and Sarah, but now the only thing the children could think about was Mr Linden.

'Can Jamie stay tonight?' John suddenly asked.

Dad looked surprised but he didn't say no. 'We'll have to see. Would you like to, Jamie?'

'Oh, yes please, Mr Ward,' Jamie said.

'Deserting me already?' Uncle Chris laughed.

'We wanted to do some work on our project,' Jamie said, 'and you could come and pick me up tomorrow.'

'Oh, could I?' Uncle Chris said. 'We'll have to see what your mum says.'

Mrs Ward phoned Jamie's mum, who was only too happy for Jamie to stay if he wasn't any bother, and then found a pair of John's pyjamas for Jamie to wear. Uncle Chris left Jamie at the Wards' house after tea, looking happier than he'd been for months.

Up in the tree house, with the whole evening before them, the children had a chance to plan their next move. Jamie was given the identikit picture to look at and he read every detail carefully. He took his turn at the window on lookout without a murmur and was rewarded by getting the first glimpse of Mr Linden returning from the coast.

Jamie relayed every movement to the twins, who craned their necks to get a view over his shoulders.

'He's coming round the side of the house, he's still got the sack, he's putting it down, it's on the lawn. He's undoing it, no, he's not. The spade's covered in mud. He's put it down. He's going inside!'

'If only we knew what was in the sack,' Sarah said.

'It could be all the proof we need,' John agreed.

Jamie scratched his head, then he sat bolt upright and looking at them, eyes sparkling. 'Let's go and look.'

'What!' the twins cried in disbelief.

'Why not?'

'We can't just troop round there.'

'Listen, I've got a plan. We drop a football over the fence, then you,' he pointed at Sarah, 'go to Mr Linden's front door and ring the bell. You ask if you can get your ball back. While you're talking, we nip round the side, have a look in the sack and get back. You keep him talking. . . .'

'What about?'

'Anything! You're neighbours, you can think of something, just to give us a minute, that's all we'll need. And then you get the ball so he's not suspicious. Easy!'

Five minutes later a very reluctant Sarah was being pushed and coaxed up to the front door of next door's house.

'This is the worst bit,' Sarah argued. 'It's not fair.'

'You'll be much better at talking than either of us and anyway he won't get cross at you for chucking the ball over,' John explained.

Sarah still hesitated but when Jamie said, 'Oh, *I'll* do it then,' she plucked up enough courage to ring the bell.

The boys fled and she was left trembling on the doorstep, wondering what on earth she was going to say. Sarah heard heavy footsteps and then a lock being unbolted before the door swung open, to reveal Mr Linden.

He had changed into jeans and a sweater and he must have had a shower because his hair was still damp and sticking to his head.

'Oh, excuse me, but can I have my football back – it's in your garden,' Sarah stammered.

Mr Linden looked down at her. 'Aren't you from next door?' he said.

'Yes, that's right.'

'You'd be Sarah, then.'

'Yes.'

'Well, you must be a good football player to have kicked a ball all that way.'

'I'm not bad. John's even better though,' Sarah blurted out, remembering that she was supposed to be spinning this out a bit.

'I'll bet he isn't,' Mr Linden smiled. 'Well, off you go, then.'

'Thank you very much,' Sarah said. She paused on the doorstep trying to think of something else to say but her mind went blank.

'Is there anything else?' Mr Linden said.

'Oh, no-um, thanks,' and Sarah dashed round

the side. She saw the ball, grabbed it and ran. The boys were gone so they must have managed their bit. When she got back to the front of the house the front door had already closed.

He didn't really seem like a criminal, Sarah thought as she trudged back up her drive. She darted past the kitchen window but Mum and Dad weren't in there anyway. She couldn't wait to learn what John and Jamie had discovered.

They were sitting cross-legged on the floor of the tree house.

'Well?' Sarah demanded.

They looked up at her rather blankly.

'Oh, stop messing around, John, what did you find in the sack?' Sarah said, crossly.

'This,' John said. In his hand was a plant. It had a small bulb, with knobbly bits all over it and soil still clinging to the roots which were coarse and hairy. The stem was a bit crushed but the leaves were pale green, clearly veined and the flower, which had partly died, was a deep purple with yellow spots.

'Is that *all*?' Sarah said, incredulously.

'There were several more of the same plants,' Jamie said.

'You mean I went to all that bother just for you to discover a sack full of weeds!' Sarah felt very hard done by. 'What a waste of time,' she said.

'What is it?' Jamie asked.

'It's a weed!' Sarah said.

'It's a wild flower,' John corrected her, 'and I don't know what sort.'

'Hm,' Jamie fingered the leaves. 'I don't suppose

your mum would know, would she?'

'Well, she might,' John said, 'but then she'd want to know where we'd seen it and we can't tell her about going next door.'

'She's got a great big flower book,' Sarah said, suddenly remembering.

'Go and get it.'

Sarah went inside to find the book. When she returned, John and Jamie spent a long time flicking through the pages. They dismissed all the common ones easily but at last Jamie stabbed his finger on a picture.

'That's not the right colour,' he said, 'but it's definitely the shape.'

'There's more over the page,' Sarah said. 'It's an orchid.'

Slowly now, the boys turned each page in the orchid section searching for the colour and the shape as they compared the real but wilting flower with the photographs. When they saw it, both knew at once that they were sure.

Sarah whipped the book away from them and started to read the description of habitat and seasons of growth.

'Except for one or two locations the habitat of this flower has almost disappeared on mainland Britain,' she read.

'Do you mean to say that Mr Linden has found the rare orchids on the cliffs?'

'It looks like it,' Jamie said.

'But you're not allowed to pick rare wild flowers,' Sarah said, remembering her nature lessons at school.

'He's not just picking them, he's digging them up by the sackful!' Jamie said.

John was serious and thoughtful now. 'We've got to catch him in the act of digging them up and report him! It'll be our best case of detective work yet.'

Chapter Seven

'Don't you mind going to church?' Jamie asked, as they got ready next morning.

'No, it's all right – in fact it's quite good sometimes,' John said, tugging at his shoelace.

Jamie scowled, not convinced. 'It's boring and soppy,' he said.

'It wouldn't be if you listened and joined in,' Sarah said.

'But it's not real, is it?'

'Of course it's real,' Sarah replied.

'Mum used to make me say prayers every night but I don't any more, not since Dad . . . went away.'

'Why?' John asked simply.

'Because it didn't help. They still put my dad in prison.'

It was the first time Jamie had talked about his dad and the twins weren't quite sure what to say.

'God loves your dad, even in prison, because

God loves everyone, so you could still pray that your dad's all right,' John suggested.

Jamie was silent.

'I bet today's lesson will be some daft story about people in olden times,' he finally announced.

'What's wrong with that?' Sarah asked. She liked some of the stories from the Old Testament although they did seem to fight each other quite a lot.

'It's got nothing to do with going to school or homework, has it? I mean there's never anything about ordinary people.'

John was just going to argue about that when Mum and Dad called them all downstairs, and there wasn't any time to talk.

Jamie was wrong about one thing anyway, because the lesson was mostly about getting ready for Harvest festival. The theme that year, their teacher said, was looking after God's creation. They had to jot down all the animals they could think of which were dying out and then try to suggest reasons why this was happening. It didn't take long to make a list, or for the children to come up with the sad conclusion that it was mostly man's fault that several species would soon be extinct. Hunting animals and cutting down their homes seemed to be the main causes.

'Could plants become extinct too?' Sarah asked.

John and Jamie gave her a warning look not to give anything away, but the teacher didn't notice.

'Oh yes, Sarah, that's why it's part of the country code not to pick some wild flowers. And of course some trees are quite rare now. But what I want us to think about today is how God feels about the way we look after the world. Let's just read a bit from the Bible to help us.'

Sarah and John had heard the story about God making the world, and Noah's Ark, when they were very little, but today their teacher read the verses where God put man in charge of all the plants and animals.

'Now,' she said, 'do you think God wants us to do just as we please with his creation?'

'I think he wants us to look after the animals,' Emma Parsons said.

'We can still eat them though, that's what it says,' Jamie pointed out.

'Yes,' Paul agreed, 'but as long as you don't eat too many, they breed and replace the ones that we kill.'

The discussion wandered off into whether everyone ought to be a vegetarian but the teacher said that was a matter of personal choice. 'Jesus ate fish and meat,' she reminded them.

'We ought to care for the world, or it'll be all messed up in a few years time,' Emma said, very seriously.

'How can we do anything?' Louise asked.

'There are lots of little things we can do,' their teacher explained, 'like looking after our own pets properly, and feeding our wild birds during winter. We can remember not to drop litter and, when you're a little older, you may want to join societies who try to protect species of animals.'

There was a lot of chat and ideas about looking after nature. Time ran out before half of them had been properly talked about so their teacher promised they could spend next week's lesson on the same subject. At the end, they closed their eyes while their teacher prayed. She thanked God for giving them such a beautiful world and mentioned some of the animals who were in danger. It had been a very interesting lesson, and even Jamie had to admit it was OK.

'We could really do something about it if we could get Mr Linden caught for stealing all those flowers,' John said, as they waited for their parents, who were busy talking as usual.

'It means being on the cliff as he returns with the sack, and having an adult there at the same time.'

'The coastguards!' Sarah said. 'They'd be interested in our discovery, and it's part of their job to look after the coast. They'd be bound to take us seriously.'

'But how do we know when Mr Linden will go back up there, and then how do we persuade our parents to let us follow, without telling them why we need to be there?' Jamie sighed.

'Mum and Dad would never let us just follow Mr Linden, and we can't tell them about the sack, not yet.'

'What about if we found the place where he'd dug them up?' Jamie suggested. 'Then we'd have the evidence to prove that it was the rare orchid he was digging up and that ought to be enough proof for the coastguard.'

'Why not tell Mum and Dad now?' Sarah asked.

'Because they'd just ask Mr Linden about it, and he'd deny it. Anyway we want to solve this case all on our own,' John said firmly.

'Too right,' Jamie agreed.

'Well, you'll have to persuade Mum and Dad to take us up there again,' Sarah said. She didn't think there was much chance, seeing as Dad had spent the whole of the previous afternoon up there.

Jamie's mum and Uncle Chris were waiting to take him home but he seemed so reluctant to leave the twins that the two adults were persuaded to join the Wards for lunch.

'Great!' Jamie said.

'I hope Jamie isn't outstaying his welcome,' Mrs Clark said anxiously.

'Not in the least. They've been as good as gold together. I believe the project is really coming on,' Mrs Ward said.

'Yes, we just need another visit to the station,' Jamie put in, taking the opportunity, 'so that Sarah can sketch it properly.'

'Oh, I don't know . . .' Mrs Clark said, 'it would be nice just to put my feet up this afternoon.'

'Don't worry, I'll play chauffeur again,' Uncle Chris said.

'Really? Oh, that'd be great!' Jamie said.

'I've never seen you so excited about doing school work,' Mrs Clark laughed.

Jamie calmed down and tried to look offhand about whether or not they were going but he couldn't hide his impatience.

Back at home, the house was so full that the children easily escaped to the tree house to plan the afternoon.

'You'll have to do a sketch, Sarah,' John said,

'because that's the whole reason why we're going, as far as Uncle Chris knows.'

'That's not fair! I'll miss all the fun stuck up there. Why can't Jamie do it?'

'I can't draw!' Jamie grinned.

For once Sarah wished she couldn't either. She looked down at the shrivelled up orchid lying where they had left it and felt a bit guilty.

'It's dead,' she said.

'Only the flower,' Jamie replied. 'My mum digs up her tulip bulbs every year and then she plants them in the spring and they shoot again.'

'Wild orchids don't get dug up, though,' Sarah pointed out.

'Let's plant it then!' John suggested.

'Where?'

'In our herb garden!'

The twins had been given a special bit of the garden where they could grow whatever they liked, on condition that they did all the weeding. It was a bit overgrown and untidy because their original interest had worn off a bit.

Sarah thought about the morning's lesson as she dug a small hole with the trowel. They hadn't been able to stop Mr Linden from digging up the orchids but at least they could make sure this one had a chance. It wasn't quite the same as growing on a cliff-side but perhaps it would still grow the lovely mauve flowers next year. John patted the soil down carefully and they stuck a little twig in to the mark the spot.

'I wonder what he's going to do with all the plants still in the sack?' John said.

They couldn't really think of a reasonable answer.

'Perhaps he just wants them growing in his own garden,' Jamie said.

'That's really greedy! That means no-one else can see them,' Sarah said.

'He had loads though! Perhaps he's going to sell them. They'd be worth an awful lot if they're so rare.'

After lunch it seemed as if Uncle Chris would never stop drinking coffee. The children cleared the table, helped wash up and got ready without being told to, but still the adults chatted.

Jamie ended up almost dragging his uncle out of his chair.

Mr Ward looked out of the window. 'Hm, looks like rain. Have you all got anoraks?'

'Yes, come on, let's go,' Jamie said. If it actually started to rain before they left there would be all sorts of reasons why they shouldn't go.

Once on his feet, Uncle Chris was quick to get ready and head towards the car.

'You all be very careful,' Mum shouted. 'No wandering off up there.'

'Don't worry, we'll be good,' John said, before he closed the door firmly behind him. It had started to drizzle and the children were terrified that Uncle Chris would call the trip off but he didn't seem quite so fussy as their mums were. His old car growled to life and they were soon bumping along on the sagging suspension. They parked near the coastguard station and the children scrambled out.

'Stay on the track,' Uncle Chris warned.

'We will.'

'See you in about an hour?' he called, settling himself down.

'Oh yes, that should do it,' John said.

'Don't worry, he'll never notice the time once he gets his nose into the newspaper,' Jamie said as they set off.

Sarah insisted that the boys stayed with her while she sketched the station and they reluctantly agreed. Jamie thought it was only fair, and John realised that his sister might not go along with the plan if he left her. It took about a quarter of an hour for Sarah to draw a reasonable likeness of the station. She would spend hours at home shading it in, but at least the basic shape had been captured. She folded the paper carefully and tucked it inside her anorak. They were all feeling a bit cold just from standing around. The clouds had come down and you couldn't really see very far. The headland was a misty blur and the cows had turned their backs on the wind and lowered their heads. It was a miserable afternoon compared to the previous day.

'I wonder how many ships will get lost out there today?' Sarah said as they trudged towards the cliff path.

'I'm cold!' Jamie grumbled, tucking his chin inside the collar of his anorak.

'Come on,' John ordered, 'we haven't got any time to mess around.' He started to jog in the direction of the ridge where they'd seen Mr Linden yesterday.

Drops of rain had collected on the leaves of the gorse bushes and when John brushed past them they sprayed water all over Jamie and Sarah.

Underfoot the path was soggy and the grass very slippery. Twice Sarah nearly crashed into Jamie as she skidded. It was very tiring walking against the wind. Sometimes it was so strong that they felt themselves being shoved sideways off the path.

'We need to go down more,' John said, suddenly stopping.

'The path curves round though,' Sarah said.

'I know, that's why we've got to get off it.'

'John, we're not allowed to,' Sarah said, remembering all the things Dad had said about staying on the path.

'It's all right, Sarah,' John said. 'We can see where we're going and I only want to get as far as Mr Linden was yesterday.'

'He had a rope,' Sarah put in.

'Well, we aren't going to climb rocks. Look, see down there? It's only a little way. If we get to there and we can't see any signs of digging we'll come back up. OK?'

Sarah peered down. It didn't look too bad. 'All right, but no further.'

'It's a bit steep,' Jamie muttered. 'Aaggh!' His foot suddenly skidded from under him, he grabbed at Sarah's arm and they both slid several yards on their backsides before crashing into a gorse bush which stopped their fall.

'Oo, my arm!' Jamie said.

'I've got prickles everywhere!' Sarah moaned. 'Why did you knock me over?'

'I couldn't help it.'

'Look at my jeans. I'm soaking wet.'

John stared at them as they sorted themselves

out, tapping his foot impatiently.

'Honestly, you two,' he said.

'I knew we shouldn't have left the path,' Sarah said.

'The ground just gives way,' Jamie said. 'Look!' He kicked at some loose stones which went hurtling down dragging quite a lot of soil with them. 'It's like a mini avalanche everytime you put your foot down.'

John wasn't put off. 'You've got to expect a bit of difficulty if you're a detective,' he explained. 'We've only got about the length of our garden to go. Come on.'

Still moaning, Sarah and Jamie struggled to their feet.

'You go ahead this time,' Sarah insisted. 'It's *my* turn to fall on top of you.'

It may have looked like the length of their garden but it turned out to be quite a lot further by the time the children reached the lower track. Even the cows didn't wander down this far. The ground levelled off here and then you met a barbed wire fence which marked the limit of the cliff line. Beneath this was a drop of about a hundred metres to the sea. They could hear the waves crashing below them and the wind was full of salt spray which they could taste on their lips.

'Look at this!' John cried excitedly. There were places all around where the soil had been disturbed, quite recently by the looks of things.

'This is where he came all right,' Jamie said. 'We've found the place!'

'Can we remember how to get here again?'

'Yes, of course. All we need to do is find an orchid, if there are any left, and then go and report the whole story to the coastguard. Mr Linden's going to get a nasty shock when he gets fined.'

'And what a brilliant story for our project!' Sarah said.

'Come on then, spread out, on your hands and knees and find the orchids.'

Staying well back from the barbed wire, and feeling a lot safer on the level surface, the children separated a bit to cover more ground. They had searched unsuccessfully for several minutes before Jamie gave a shout from around a bit of cliff which jutted out a long way beyond the wire fence.

'Have you found one?' Sarah said, hurrying towards him.

Jamie didn't answer but as the twins pushed closer, he held up his discovery in both hands. It was a sack. Not just a sack, but *the* sack. Next to it in the grass was a coil of rope. They weren't very wet so must have been dropped there quite recently.

'He's here!' John whispered.

'Where?' Sarah gulped, looking over her shoulder in alarm.

'Not here exactly, but somewhere not too far away. He must be. Quick, look in the sack.'

'Nothing!' Jamie said, shaking the bag to prove it.

'He must still be looking, then.'

'No wonder we can't find any orchids. He must be planning to steal every single one.'

'If they're that rare, there can't be many left even

for Mr Linden to find.'

'I don't want to meet him right here,' Sarah said.
She was beginning to feel a bit nervous. It was
one thing chasing a criminal but catching one red-
handed was a bit different.

For once John agreed.

'Let's get back up the cliff, get your Uncle Chris
and then report to the coastguard.'

'Right!' Jamie said. 'Shall we leave the sack?'

'No, we'll take it. It's all evidence. It proves he's
up to something.'

'What about the rope?' Sarah said.

'We'll take that too,' Jamie said, throwing it over
his shoulder.

'I wonder why he left them?' Sarah asked.

John shrugged his shoulders.

'You don't think he's gone over the barbed wire,
do you?' Jamie asked.

Sarah shuddered at the idea. He wouldn't do
that without a rope, she thought. Would he?

'Come on let's get back,' John said.

The sooner they fetched the coastguards the
better. If Mr Linden was over the fence he really
was stupid.

As the children turned away from the cliff edge
the wind dropped for a moment. They could hear
the waves again and some gulls were screeching in
the sky above them. They were making a fantastic
noise. John stared up at them. They were wheeling
round and round in great circles. Then, in the
middle of all their noise the children heard something which made them stop. They weren't quite
sure but then it came again. It was a man's voice,

shouting for help, but from a long way off.

John spun round, looking left and right, but no-one was in sight.

'It came from that way, I think,' Sarah said, very softly, pointing.

They moved slowly over to the right, afraid of making too much noise in case they missed the cry for help.

'What are we going to do?' Jamie was saying.

'Sh!' John interrupted as the cry came again.

'Help! Someone help!' It sort of trailed off at the end into a gasp, as if the person was in pain or very tired.

'Let's get back to Uncle Chris,' Jamie said in a frightened voice.

'We've got to find out where he is first,' Sarah said.

'It's Mr Linden,' John said. 'It's got to be.'

'Serves him right,' Jamie muttered.

The twins didn't reply. If Mr Linden had got himself stuck without a rope it probably did serve him right but even so, they'd got to help him now.

'Let's all shout together,' Sarah said. 'Ready? One, two, three . . . Mr Linden!!'

They screamed into the wind, cupping their mouths with their hands.

They waited for what seemed like several moments but then the cry came back, much stronger.

'Over here!'

The children could definitely pinpoint the sound now. Mr Linden *had* gone over the barbed wire fence, at the point where Jamie found the sack.

'Hold on, Mr Linden,' John cried out.

'You're not going over there!' Jamie said as John hooked his toe on the bottom rung of the fence.

'We've got to see where he is.'

'Tie the rope round your waist,' Sarah said.

'Yeah, that'll be safer,' Jamie agreed.

They tied the rope carefully around John's waist, left enough for him to walk to the cliff edge and then tied the other end around one of the fence posts.

Jamie pulled the knot tight and then he and Sarah braced themselves against the fence with the rope in their hands just in case the knot gave way.

Very slowly, testing each step as if he might be treading on land mines, John made his way towards the edge. His heart was beating so hard it was making his throat ache. About a metre away from empty space he got down onto his stomach, wriggling inch by inch until he could look down.

His stomach lurched and his hands were so tightly gripped into the grassy tufts that the knuckles were white.

'Mr Linden?' he called.

'Over here. I'm on a ledge. I can't see you.'

John scanned the ledge immediately below him and then shifted his position slightly. He had expected the cliff to fall headlong into the sea but it didn't. There were odd ledges and bits jutting out all the way down. It was here that the gulls nested. They were still screaming above, obviously upset at this very unwelcome intruder.

Mr Linden was lying flat on his back on a very narrow ledge about five metres below John. It would have been possible to climb back up but Mr Linden was obviously hurt and in a lot of pain. John was surprised that he'd even managed to get down there in the first place with his bad leg.

'We'll get help, Mr Linden!' John shouted. 'Will you be OK?'

'My legs,' the man groaned. 'They're numb. I'm so cold. I'm going giddy.'

'Mr Linden!' John was terrified of leaving the man. He didn't seem to be quite all there. Perhaps he was delirious. That sometimes happened when people were in shock – they went a bit crazy. Well, if Mr Linden rolled off the ledge. . . . It made John feel sick. He started to crawl back towards Sarah and Jamie.

Chapter Eight

'One of us ought to stay with him while the other two fetch help,' John decided as he crouched beside the fence with the others.

'Who then?' Jamie asked.

There was an awkward pause.

'Whoever can run fastest ought to fetch help,' John said.

'Well, that's you,' Sarah said rather reluctantly. She could already see who was going to be staying with Mr Linden.

'I could stay with Sarah,' Jamie volunteered.

Sarah was relieved but she knew it wasn't the best idea really. Someone had to fetch the coast-guard, someone else ought to find Uncle Chris, then he could help with the rescue.

'I'll stay here,' she said bravely, trying to disguise the tremble in her voice. She didn't dare to think of what she would do if Mr Linden fell again. 'Please hurry,' she said.

'Don't worry, we'll be back before you know it,' John said. 'Now look, tie the rope round you, like I did and just sit very still on the edge. It's safe there. Try and keep Mr Linden talking, you know, keep his spirits up. And when you see us coming start shouting so we can find you again. Right?'

'OK,' Sarah said doubtfully.

The boys started to climb back up the cliff. It was very difficult work and it was a long time before they were out of sight. Sarah knew she was going to have a long wait.

She tied the rope round her waist like John had done and started to crawl to the edge of the cliff. The wind was very strong and her teeth were chattering. She dragged the sack behind her. She had had an idea for making Mr Linden a bit more comfortable.

It took a while for Sarah to get into a position where she could see Mr Linden and still stay a little bit back from the edge, but at last she managed.

The man had propped himself on one elbow but both legs looked completely useless. He was groaning softly.

'Mr Linden, can you hear me?' Sarah cried.

'There was a pause. Mr Linden twisted his head around and squinted upwards at her. 'Fetch help!' he cried.

'It's all right, John and Jamie have gone. They won't be long. I'm going to stay with you until they get back with the coastguard. Look Mr Linden, if I throw this sack down, do you think you can catch it? It's quite thick, maybe you can put it over your legs to keep them warm.'

Mr Linden nodded and tried to shift himself up the ledge but he sank back exhausted.

Sarah folded the sack up into a tight ball, so the wind wouldn't catch it, and tried to aim before she dropped it. More by luck than anything else, the sack bounced against a rock and landed on the ledge just beside Mr Linden's head. He reached out and drew/it over his body. It was the thick hessian type of sack and would help keep the wind out a bit.

'Thank you,' he gasped, biting his lip with the pain of moving.

Sarah ignored the creeping dampness which was chilling her and tried to think of encouraging things to say. Mr Linden had his eyes closed and she was afraid that if he fell asleep he might roll off the ledge. She had to keep him awake. 'Mr Linden!'

'How do you know my name?' he suddenly called, as if the thought had only just occurred to him.

'It's me, Sarah, from next door. It was John who found you, my brother.'

'Sarah with the football?'

'Yes that's right.'

Mr Linden smiled very weakly. 'I'm a lucky man.'

'We heard you calling,' Sarah explained. 'Why were you digging the flowers up?' she added. It wasn't the right time to start questioning the man, Sarah knew, but she was desperate for things to talk about.

Mr Linden winced with pain. 'The flowers, Sarah. They're very important, very secret.'

'I know. But why did you dig them up?' Sarah couldn't keep the scolding tone out of her voice.

'They have to be protected, Sarah,' Mr Linden said, and he was really earnest now, in spite of his pain. 'I wanted to spread them all around the coast again. This is a special place. Nobody knows about it. My friends . . . they can spread the bulbs in special places all over the country. The orchid can grow again in Scotland, and Wales. I just needed a few more bulbs. . . .'

'Is that why you went over the fence?' Sarah asked.

'Yes, I thought I could get back up but my leg gave way and I fell. Nobody must know about the orchids, Sarah. Please. . . .'

Mr Linden seemed to be getting in such a state that Sarah quickly promised that she wouldn't say a word to anyone. She didn't quite understand, but it seemed as if Mr Linden wasn't a criminal after all, not completely, anyway.

He was groaning again and saying one or two things that didn't make sense. Sarah shivered and wished the boys would come back.

'You go that way, get your uncle, I'll go on to the coastguard station,' John gasped.

Jamie nodded, took a great breath of air and ran on.

John felt as if his lungs were going to burst. They'd run up hill practically all the way. He was hot in spite of the wind and rain, and his fringe was plastered against his forehead. The station was a tiny white block like a piece of lego on the horizon.

116

It didn't seem possible that his legs would ever carry him there. John put his head down and watched his mud-streaked trainers as they appeared, one by one in front of him, as if his legs were automatic. There was a searing pain in his side which he tried to ignore. He tried to count his steps in fifties but eventually he just forced himself to think of nothing except the station. If only he could get there, everything would be all right.

The journey which seemed never ending at last was beaten. John raised his head and saw the coastguard station clearly. He could even see a figure moving behind the windows. The car park at this end was deserted. Putting on one last spurt John reached the door and collapsed against it, banging with his feet and fists.

It suddenly gave way and he half fell, half clambered inside.

'There's been an accident! On the cliffs . . . Mr Linden . . . Sarah . . .' He couldn't get the words out he was so exhausted.

'Now lad, take a breath.' It was Jim's deep voice. John was scooped into a chair and someone dragged his soaking anorak off.

'What's happened? Two people injured you say?'

'No, no. It's Mr Linden, he's fallen over the cliff. I think he's broken his leg. He's on a ledge and he can't move. My sister, Sarah, is with him.'

'On the ledge?'

'No, she's on the edge of the cliff but she's OK.'

'Sounds like a job for the Helicopter Rescue. Get on to RAF Freymer, Alan!' The younger man snatched up a phone.

There was another knock on the door as Jamie and his uncle arrived.

'Anything I can do?' Chris asked. He looked worried and was holding onto Jamie's shoulder tightly.

'I'll alert the emergency services to stand by,' Jim said, 'but we need to give an accurate location for the helicopter crew. Come and look at this map, boys.'

John and Jamie stared at the map until their eyes hurt but things looked so different on paper.

'It might be easier to walk back,' Uncle Chris suggested.

'Are you up to it, boys?'

Just a few minutes previously, John would have said he couldn't ever walk another step but now that the responsibility for Mr Linden was taken off his shoulders he thought he could probably make the return journey. Anyway, he suddenly thought of Sarah waiting for them in the cold.

Jim collected emergency equipment, the boys grabbed wet-weather gear and they set out. Jim had a walkie-talkie so he could maintain contact with Alan who could give the helicopter crew better information. The weather had worsened. They would have to be quick or an air resuce might not be possible.

'Please, God, make them come,' Sarah said softly. Mr Linden had gone very quiet and still. She was too afraid to shout down to him and too stiff with the cold to move. It seemed like hours since John and Jamie had left her. Where were they? Even the gulls had quietened down. Sarah couldn't see much

118

in any direction. She was soaked to the skin. There was a dull throbbing noise in the sky above which increased until it settled a little way out to sea. It was a small speck in the air which slowly increased in size until she could feel the downsweep of the helicopter blades pushing her closer to the ground. It was the rescue team, at last. Sarah staggered to her feet and waved her arms wildly, stepping well back from the edge. The helicopter banked towards her and then hovered over her head. She could even see the pilot waving back to her. A side door slid back and a man with a stretcher stepped over the side into nothingness. He was winched down and down.

'Oh, Mr Linden!' Sarah shouted. 'It's OK. They're here. You're safe!'

'Sarah!' It was John's voice and he was running towards her. Sarah rushed back to the fence where Uncle Chris was waiting to lift her over. There was a crackling sound as the pilot radioed to Jim on the ground and Jim replied. John and Jamie were both talking over each other and Sarah was too relieved to say anything.

When they saw Mr Linden strapped onto the stretcher being winched back towards the helicopter everyone cheered. The helicopter hovered for a moment and then lurched away. The rescue was complete.

The children were so tired that they could hardly put one foot in front of the other. There was an ambulance waiting at the station and Jim insisted that the children had a quick check over. They were cold, tired and in need of a good hot bath but none the worse for their adventure. By this time Mr and Mrs Ward had driven up with Mrs Clark and everyone had to start talking and explaining all over again.

'Another one of these ill-equipped walkers,' Jim said, scribbling notes in his pad.

'Well, I . . .' Jamie began but Sarah interrupted him.

'Yes, that's right,' she said firmly.

'It's lucky you just happened to spot him,' Jim continued.

'What were you doing down there?' Mr Ward wanted to know.

'It's a long story, Dad,' John said.

'Which can wait until tomorrow,' Mrs Ward said very firmly.

The children were glad to climb into the car and think of hot chocolate drinks.

'What do you mean we're not going to use the story?' John cried, amazed. He and Jamie stared at Sarah across the school desk as if she was mad.

'Shh!' she said, glancing over her shoulder. 'Someone might hear.'

The boys gave in.

The project was going ahead brilliantly. The rescue had been in the local paper with a write-up so everyone at school knew about their adventure. What they didn't know about was Mr Linden's discovery and their plan to catch him digging up the rare orchids. The children now knew that his motives hadn't been criminal of course. It turned out that he was a member of a society for finding and studying flowers all over Britain. Mr Linden's plan for redistributing the rare flowers was already under way. The bulbs had been posted off to horticulturalists in Scotland, Wales and Yorkshire who were supposed to find suitable places in their areas to plant the bulbs. But that was what John and Jamie wanted to add to the project. As far as they were concerned it would make a perfect ending, and the prize for the best project would be theirs.

'Don't you want to win?' John said later, as they sat in the dining room putting the finishing touches to their work. Jamie had stayed to tea so that he could help.

'Of course I want to win, but it wouldn't be fair.'

'Why not?'

'On Mr Linden I mean.'

'I don't understand.'

'I promised him that we wouldn't tell anyone about the flowers. If we write it all up, everyone in our class will know; they'll tell all their parents. The next thing you know there'll be people stomping all over the cliffs trying to find this rare orchid. There won't be any left in this area and Mr Linden said it's a very important growing place. He said it's the only place in the whole country where they actually thrive.'

The boys thought about this. Sarah sensed her advantage and pushed it home. 'We all talked about looking after God's creation last Sunday. Well, this is one way we can help. If we're just greedy for the prize you can tell everyone but if we keep this a special secret, we'll be looking after the orchid in the best way we can.' Sarah paused. 'It's up to you.

If you both want to use the story it's two against one.' Sarah was fair, even in a case like this.

John sighed. He had been very tempted but since Sarah put it like that . . . he thought he knew what God would prefer him to do. 'What do you say, Jamie?'

Jamie looked at the twins. He'd learnt a lot of things recently. He had realised that silly lies and boasts didn't get you friends, but being thoughtful and kind did. They could boast about their brilliant detective work but this was more important. 'The case is closed,' he smiled. 'Operation Orchid is now an official secret.'

The case wasn't quite closed though. Mr Linden arrived home from hospital the next day. He was on crutches and one hand was bandaged up but he sent a message round almost at once, asking if the three children could visit him on an important matter.

After school, as they stood at his front door. Sarah remembered the first time she'd knocked when they'd thought he was a criminal and she'd been so afraid.

Mr Linden opened the door and ushered them inside.

'Come on in, my brave rescuers!' he smiled.

They felt a bit uncomfortable. Mr Linden knew that the only reason that they'd found him that day was because they'd been watching him and snooping around his house.

'First of all, a small token of my thanks,' he said, handing each one of them a crisp five pound note. They weren't quite sure whether they should accept such a large amount of money but Mr Linden insisted.

'I might not be here today, if it hadn't been for your courage and sense. Anyway, that's not the main reason why I asked you round. I may have a job for you.'

The children looked at each other in surprise. What could they possibly do for Mr Linden?

'I think you're perfect for what I've got in mind; observant, brave, loyal and above all, you can keep a secret!' Sarah blushed with pride.

'Look here.' Mr Linden crossed to a drawer, opened it and took out a small brown envelope.

'This was posted to me last week. It contains a small quantity of a valuable seed.'

'Another rare flower?' Sarah said.

'Not rare exactly, but special to me. I used to see these poppies any time I liked in the fields and along the hedgerows where I lived as a child. Pesticides have killed a lot of them but now that farmers are using different methods, poppies are becoming much more common. I'd like to introduce them around here. In my own garden for a start and the fields just behind your school. They need to be scattered now but as you can see . . .' Mr Linden looked down at his crutches and made a face. 'I won't be doing much more than hobbling around indoors for a few weeks.'

'You want us to plant the seeds?' Jamie said.

'If you think you can,' Mr Linden said.

'Of course we can!' John said. He could already see them planning the operation. They'd have to make it a secret operation, of course. . . .

'When shall we start?' Sarah said.

'Right away if you like,' Mr Linden said.

'Well, if you get any more special deliveries that need dealing with, you know where to come,' John said in his detective voice.

'I certainly do, young man.'

'Brilliant!' John said when they were back home. 'We'll be advertising our services soon. "Ward and Clark, private detectives".'

'I think I might like to be a gardener when I grow up,' Sarah said thoughtfully.

John raised his eyes to the sky. Jamie just smiled. The twins, he suddenly realised, were the best friends he'd ever had.

It was over a fortnight later that the awards for the projects were made. It was a special occasion and all the junior children were gathered into the hall for an assembly.

Mr Wykes, the headmaster, gave a long speech congratulating everyone on how much effort they'd put into their projects and then he held up the winning folder and read out the names. It was a project on 'Water and Sewage Works' by Tim and Matthew. They went up to the front to collect their book tokens and everyone clapped. Jamie and the twins clapped extra hard, partly to cover their disappointment and partly because it was a very good project and deserved to win.

Then the headmaster held up his hands for silence.

'There was another project which attracted a lot of attention.' The headmaster paused while the murmurs quietened down. 'We have some visitors today who would like to make an award of their own. Please welcome Mr Wilcox and Mr Taylor from the Coastguard Station.'

Jim looked different in his smart uniform and with his tie straight. He also seemed a bit nervous, but once he got started he was just as they knew him.

The twins and Jamie were cheered as they received special badges with the coastguard emblem on them.

'This project may not have won the prize,' Jim said, waving their folder in the air, 'but it shows how important the coastguards are and we are going to use a copy of this project to help us in our campaign to keep your local station open.'

Jamie and the twins returned to their places holding their badges proudly. It was the first thing Jamie had ever won, as far as he could remember, and he was delighted.

When the twins were sitting in their tree house after school they couldn't help laughing at the way things had turned out. Jamie, whom they'd hated, was now their best friend and Mr Linden, the criminal, was one of the nicest people they knew.

'I suppose God knows everyone just the way they are,' Sarah suddenly said as she took down the Identikit picture of Mr Linden.

'That must make him the best detective in the world,' John said.

'I think I'd like to be a Sunday School teacher when I grow up,' Sarah said.

Some other Tiger books which you might like to read. . . .

Smugglers' Cove
Pat Coleman
Seb and Fiona are spending their summer holidays at their grandmother's house. They make friends with Mike and Peter and together go exploring the caves along the coast. Mike and Peter have heard stories of smugglers in bygone days and want to find the cave they used. After a frightening incident on the beach they discover that Peter has more than his fair share of problems and they determine to help him find a way round them.

The Fen Street Flyer
Graham Jones
Another amusing story about Paul, Oliver, Richard, Eddie and the other characters in *The Bike*. As a joke, Paul and Oliver are nominated to take part in a talent contest for a TV show. Their performance is a disaster but as a result the organisers discover the Fen Street Rock Calypso band and invite them on the show. Then their instruments are stolen just before the show. Paul decides to do some investigating, starting with Eddie.

The Inca Trail
Vivien Whitfield

A collection of stories about children in Peru whose lives are very different from ours. Roberto is a shepherd up in the mountains who wants to get away to the town. Lisbet lives in a shanty town and has never seen the sea until she goes to camp. Luis is a guide to the tourists who come to visit the Inca ruins.

The Shell Box
Carol Oldham

It is the summer holidays and Laura and Tim are looking forward to a seaside holiday with their cousins, Mark and Alice. Then Theresa is fostered with Laura's family and Laura becomes very possessive of her, resenting Mark's attempts to be friendly to Theresa and imagining he is trying to get her away from Laura. When Theresa is lost one day, Mark gets the blame and he decides to make a shell box for Theresa to show he is sorry. Laura takes the box before he can give it to Theresa and hides it. Then things really start to go wrong.

Operation Sandy
Cathie Bartlam

Mick is very fond of the little puppy, Sandy, which

is being trained as a guide dog by his friend John's family. He cannot have a dog of his own so he plans to run away with Sandy. He hides in a caravan but is not sorry to be found and taken home again.

Later Nick begins to understand why Sandy could never be his dog.